I0586632

Also by Marilyn Ludwig

THE BORROWED DAYS

MARILYN LUDWIG

THE BORROWED DAYS by Marilyn Ludwig
Copyright © 2018 by Marilyn Ludwig

All rights reserved.

No part of this publication may be reproduced, stored in a retrieval system or transmitted in any form or by any means, including electronic or mechanical. Photocopying, recording or otherwise reproducing any portion of this work without the prior written permission of the author is prohibited except for brief quotations used in a review.

Book cover and interior designed by Ellie Searl, Publishista®
Maps courtesy of Jon Ludwig

ISBN-13: 9780996742269
LCCN: 2018912664

ZAFA PUBLISHING
Downers Grove, Illinois

For Sandra Mary MacLean Pavillard,
who started in Scotland, traveled the world,
and finally returned to the home of her ancestors.
And who never spoils a good story for the lack of telling it.

For Jon Ludwig, born on November 5 and able to recite the Guy
Fawkes poem. And in memory of Mary Thale, who shared the
Fifth of November birthday.

And always for Nancy,
who thought the combination of Scotland and
The Spanish Armada was both weird and wonderful.

The worst blast comes on the Borrowing Days.

March borrowed of April,
Three days, they say;
One rained, the other snowed,
And the other was the first day that ever blowed.
—Staffordshire Rhyme

March borrows from April
Three days and they are ill;
April returns them back again,
The days and they are rain.
March does from April gain
Three days and they're in rain,
Returned by April in bad kind,
Three days and they're in wind.
—Scottish Rhyme

"Those who are much addicted to superstition
will neither borrow nor lend on any of these days."
—Dr. Jamieson, Etymological Dictionary of the Scottish Language,
    1808

Major sites mentioned in *The Borrowed Days*

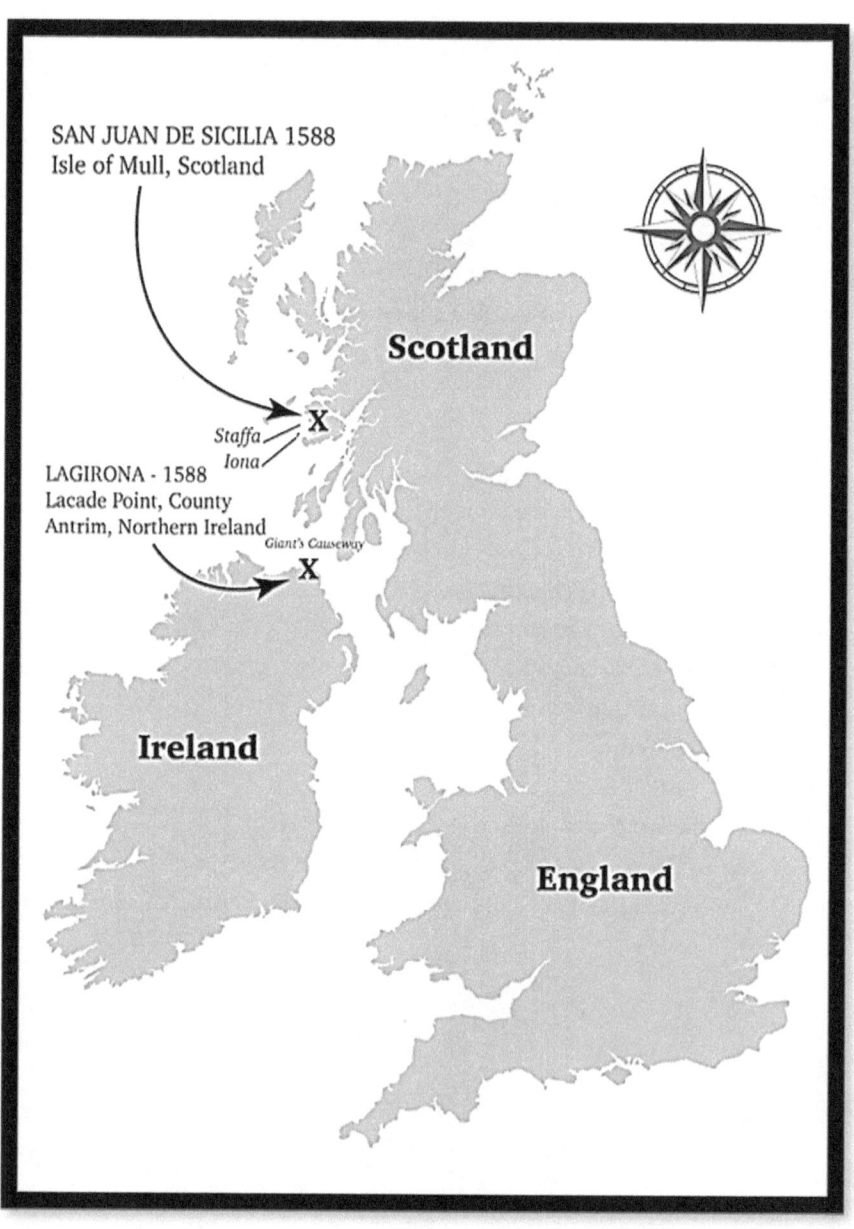

The route of the Spanish Armada

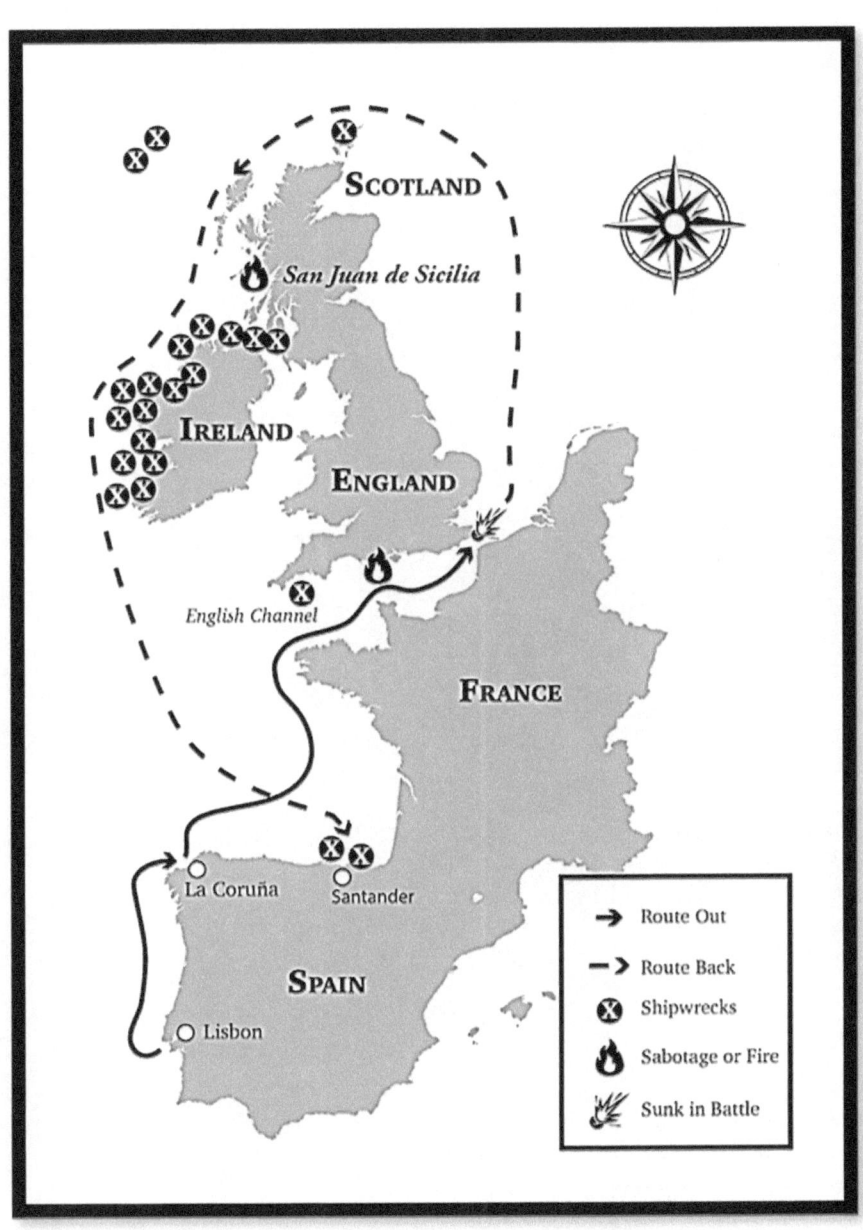

SCOTLAND

San Juan de Sicilia

IRELAND

ENGLAND

English Channel

FRANCE

La Coruña
Santander

SPAIN

Lisbon

➜ Route Out
-➤ Route Back
❌ Shipwrecks
🔥 Sabotage or Fire
💥 Sunk in Battle

Pauline

2004

PAULINE PROPER, THE STAFF CALLED her, even though *Miss Pauline Porter,* in impeccably rounded letters, had been dutifully entered into the registrar for over fifty years, longer than any of the staff had been employed at the Western Isles Hotel. Miss Proper—sometimes an unwitting maid called her that by mistake—was as regular a visitor as swallows to Capistrano or, far less romantic, as midges to the moor. Faithfully, each March 28, no matter the weather, the hotel's heavy wooden doors opened and Pauline entered, carrying an ancient pre-war suitcase and a brocade carpetbag holding her knitting and a few novels covered with brown paper wrappers. There was much speculation and a few wagers from the servers in the dining room about what might be concealed under those covers. The number one guess was lurid graphics for torrid romances, although that hardly seemed likely. Prying hotel maids knew the books were only tired classics, as washed out as their owner. Unknown to those determined maids, also packed in the bag—oh, so carefully—was Hope— torn, tattered, invisible, but still present. Hope. After all those years!

Miss Proper, that is Porter, first came to Tobermory with her parents when she was a girl of twenty-one, at the same time of year—end of March back in 1950—long, long ago. Many women in their mid-seventies and older still maintain a hint of youth, or at least give an impression of trying to defeat age— continuing to enjoy and participate in life—but in no way could that be said of stiff, starched Pauline. If you were to visualize the stereotype of an aged spinster, you'd be close to seeing her. A caricature: thin with ill-fitting clothes and practical shoes, mouse-gray hair gathered in a low careless bun, a pointed chin, glasses strictly serviceable. And covering her from head to foot, from shoulder to shoulder, was an ambience of unrelenting judgment. Only a select few at the Western Isles had ever seen her smile. The very image of a secretary bird, you might say—fitting, for years she had been part of a secretary pool in the City of London—but if you were to look carefully, perhaps you would see that the bird was wounded, battered too often, no longer expecting to heal. And if you didn't rush off but waited patiently, you might also discover that her eyes, if they met yours, were astonishingly beautiful—an unusual grayish blue, rimmed with a fine black line. Remain long enough to wonder if those lips were naturally pinched and thin, or if lipstick, normally an attempt to improve upon nature, was applied in such a way as to give that effect.

Once ensconced at the hotel, Pauline rarely went outside, although she spent little time in her room, the smallest, cheapest one the hotel offered. Over the course of a day, she rotated from dining room to lounge and back again. Occasionally, she ventured into the seldom-used small library on the second floor, always leaving it neater and dust free. Breakfasts, to the staff's despair, lasted Pauline most of the morning and consisted of tea, a sticky bun, and the Daily Telegraph (Scottish edition). For dinner, the special, whatever it might be, a glass of white wine, followed by creamy tea and three lumps of sugar—and the Evening Times. Forever seated at the same corner table with the best view of the bay, without ever watching the ships or the sea gulls or the many moods cast by the varying weather, this was Pauline's place, and she liked it that way. Or pretended to.

Did Pauline eat lunch? No one was quite sure. The Western Isles didn't serve a midday meal. Sheltered under her large umbrella, she did walk down the brae into town most noons, often returning with various small sacks from the Chocolate Shop.

This routine was likely to continue every late March until Pauline's eventual death—if Fate hadn't intervened. Three events, converging in time, were about to take center stage: A fruitless quest for Spanish treasure, an energetic boy descended from Scottish lairds, and finally, a naive young woman from Iowa. None of these events alone would be enough to change a damaged life, but these were The Borrowed Days. Anything might happen!

Francie

2004

LACHIE CALLED HER THE BROKEN LADY, but I thought her a selfish, mean-spirited crone—older than God and Old-Testament judgmental—sitting all alone at the best table in the Western Isles Hotel. She could have been enjoying the view of the bay, if she had bothered looking out the window. I suppose I did see her glance out a few times, only to turn back quickly and hide her face in her ever-present book or newspaper. If the dining room was full and a visitor had the nerve to approach her table, her face immediately projected a large sign—*Go Away. You Are Not Welcome*! And woe to anyone who might have arrived first, daring unwittingly to claim the sacred space! A glare was all that was needed to make even a formidable male scurry away, muttering apologies.

Our first meeting was hardly auspicious. Lachie and I had taken the ninety-mile train ride from Glasgow to Oban—an endless, exhausting ride —followed by the CalMac Ferry to Isle of Mull, and then the rickety bus to Tobermory, traveling the one-lane curvy roads with "passing places." Lachie was literally shot from guns by the time we arrived. But what would you expect from an active, bright, but possibly immature eight-year-old?

"Pow! Pow! Bang! Bang! I've got you now! You are definitely dead!"

"Hush, Lachie," I said, forcing down the hand holding an imaginary gun before looking around the austere dining room filled with people at least forty years older than I. "We want them to feed us—not arrest us. Aren't you a little old for Bang-Bang-You're-Dead games? Besides, I thought you were planning to be a treasure hunter."

The pistol disappeared into the ether, and out of the same place came an imaginary sword. "You mean, a pirate! Right ye are, lass! Call me Lachie the Lucky, Terror of Tobermory! Avast, mates! Shiver me timbers!"

I couldn't help laughing. It was a nice change to see him so enthused, completely different from the silent, sober child I'd rescued from a Glasgow boarding school. "Never mind the sword, Lachie. Divers for treasure aren't pirates."

"You're thinking of today, Francie. I'm back in 1588. There were plenty of pirates then. I'd be a Spanish pirate, if I could speak Spanish, so I guess I'll be an English one—except I sound like an American, and I'm Scottish. Back then, I don't think Scots were supposed to like the English." He sighed loudly enough to drown out the "pleasant music for fine dining" presently filling the room.

Fortunately, English and Scottish people are amazingly tolerant of children. (Certainly more so than folks back home in Iowa.) The elderly guests all smiled indulgently at us, with the exception of an unpleasant woman seated in the corner.

Then Lachie, the American pirate from New York, failing to heed his imaginary sword, promptly bumped into that corner table, upsetting a water glass and, worse, the scowling woman's serenity.

"Lachie, behave," I scolded, more to appease the woman than from anger. Even though he wasn't acting his age, Lachie *was* behaving—like a little boy who had had a long day of sitting still. It was past time for him to let out pent-up energy, but I was worried. What had I gotten myself into?

"Miss, I'm terribly sorry. He was playing pirate and didn't mean to be so rough. Lachie, tell the lady you're sorry."

"I'm sorry," he muttered. A short apology, but you could tell he meant it. He wasn't a disrespectful child. The lady ignored us and the waiter, who had rushed over to clean up the mess.

"It was dreadful of him," I said, only making matters worse, but the woman's hostility rattled me. "He has just spent hours on a train after being released from a grueling term at a boarding school where he was most unhappy. You understand, I'm sure."

"Quite," was the snippy response.

"Oh. Well, maybe you don't. I'm sorry, we won't bother you again. Come, Lachie."

Surprisingly, she had one more thing to say. "Lachie. That's an odd name for an American ruffian."

Lachie left his pirate fantasy and stood tall—sandy hair tousled, a remnant of chocolate still on his face from lunchtime—in my opinion, adorable. "I'm Lachlan Donald Maclean of Clan Maclean, returned to Duart Castle, the home of my ancestors. I'm pleased to meet you." I stifled my amusement over this unusual and unlikely display of dignity. I'd noticed it before when we were first introduced. I had also seen his father behave similarly, especially when he was wearing the tartan. I wondered if that was the way all Scotsmen acted when their clans were mentioned, whether or not they had ever lived in their "hameland."

The woman blinked before returning to her newspaper. Was it my imagination that she seemed dismayed? I led Lachie to the far side of the dining room. Once finished with the mopping up, the waiter came to our table.

"Never you mind, Miss Cummings. The lad meant no harm, even if he was a bit rowdy. But you would be wise to stay away from our Miss Proper. She's not likely to find the humor in anything." He smiled consolingly before hurrying our order to the kitchen. As friendly as he was, I'm sure he was thinking that the sooner we ate, the sooner we would be out of harm's way.

I laughed. "Miss Proper? I don't believe it. Did a name ever match a person so well?" And that's when Lachie said it.

"Poor lady. She can't help it, Francie. She's a poor, broken lady. Don't make fun of her." The waiter returned with breadsticks, which demanded Lachie's immediate and devout attention.

I looked at Miss Proper again, trying to see her through Lachie's eyes. Was she broken? Certainly there was an aura of permanent sadness about her. Perhaps Lachie was right. I was beginning to realize how perceptive he was—even though I had known him for only two weeks. I would be his nanny these last March days and possibly through the summer. The pay was good, the location fabulous, and I did have ulterior motives. As they say in old novels, I had intentions.

It wasn't just that Lachie's father was wealthy and devastatingly hot—
he led a fascinating life, one that could never take place in Bentonsport, Iowa.
Rory Maclean had come to Scotland to head the latest diving efforts for
Spanish Armada gold, rumored to be buried deep down but only 400 yards
off the pier of Tobermory's small harbor. A young widower and native of
New York State with Scottish ancestors, he had plunked his son into a rigid
English-run boarding school, while traveling back and forth to the States. I
met him through my father, a financial planner for Rory's firm.

Lachie's stint in boarding school had proved a disaster. Lonely and
miserable, he was the brunt of bullies and had failed most of his subjects. His
father despaired. What to do with the boy? My dad suggested me as a nanny
and tutor, which my friends found hilarious. *A chance for Francie to see the
world before settling down*, was the way Dad put it to Mom and me. *Let
her broaden her horizons.* She agreed. "Francie needs a change of scenery after
her recent bout of mono." Whether I had truly been ill or only sick of Iowa
hadn't been determined. Whichever, I had resisted strongly until I met the
man himself. Rory (Ruari) Donald Mor Maclean.

If my fantastic plan didn't succeed—if Rory failed to conclude I could
mean more to him than a convenient babysitter/teacher for his son—it
would be back to Iowa for me, to complete my degree in English by plowing
through boring classes, all the while plotting how I might be rescued. Figuring
that surely someday, someone would marry me for my bubbly personality,
sparkling wit, and trim figure. Then, as soon as I was certain of financial
security, I would become a famous writer, even though I had never actually
written anything. Goodness knows, I'd read a lot. That should count for
something.

So far, the plan was not working. Ever since I'd retrieved Lachie from a
school that could have been a location for a gothic horror film, I had not been
rewarded by even the sight of Rory. He was away on business all the time, in
Inverness, Glasgow, London, and other places, arranging details for the dive.
That he had a son who longed for him seemed of little importance. But I was
used to a father who hovered too much, so perhaps I wasn't one to judge.

Not only were we unsure when Rory would return, but the present
Laird of Duart Castle, also named Lachlan Maclean, preceded by a Sir, was
away. His meeting with Rory and Lachie, one they both looked forward to,
would happen at a later time. Without Rory or Sir Lachlan, Miss Porter—

Miss Proper's real name—was to be our consolation prize. We saw too much of her that evening and the following day. I was becoming increasingly wary of her staring at us whenever our paths crossed, although she didn't look disapproving anymore. The stares meant something else—something that made me uncomfortable.

Unfortunately, Lachie and I were stuck for long hours in the hotel. The weather had turned foul, and I realized finally that being there at the end of March was absolutely ridiculous. Diving for Spanish Armada gold would be a crazy venture at any time of year, but now? Absolute madness! And I, Francie Cummings, wanted to get hooked up with the madman in charge? What did that make me?

If only the weather would improve, there would be much to see throughout the island. A wealth of prehistoric monuments—burial mounds, ancient forts called Duns, and the standing stones of Dervaig. Duart Castle wasn't the only castle on Mull. There were the ruins of Pennygown, Aros, and Moy, as well as buses to take us there. I didn't know if those sites would interest Lachie or even me, but at least we'd get out of the hotel.

Both Lachie and I were suffering from boredom. He needed someplace to run and play, and I needed some alone time. Finally, the concierge took pity on us. His name was Angus Black, and while he hadn't been there as long as Miss Porter, he had been employed at the Western Isles for a long time. He set me straight on Miss Porter's name and told me a little of her history. He also took Lachie under his wing, regaling him with tales of sea serpents and shipwrecks. Some were so gory I feared they would keep him awake or cause nightmares, especially ones about "Auld Clootie," which I discovered, to my dismay, meant the devil.

In private, Angus told me more about Lachie's Broken Lady. "I heard about our 'Miss Proper' from my father. Mind ye that Blacks have served at the Western Isles time out o' mind. Da was the concierge when she first was to arrive with her parents. Aye, Da said she was a beauty in those days—not such a Baggy Aggie. Then as aft'n happens, along came a man, who stole her heart. An educated gent from Norwich. For three days, Da never saw a happier lassie. But the man left suddenly, the story goes, and took her heart with him. Her parents were that angry and marched her straight awa'. Back to America."

"Miss Porter is an American?"

"Aye. My father said the Porters were so rude the hotel went off Americans for years."

"I wonder from what state? She doesn't sound American."

"She surely does not. She returned home with her parents but didn't stay long. She settled in London, became a citizen an a' that."

"That would explain her accent," I said. "But she kept coming back here to Tobermory. Why? Why return to where you've been hurt so badly?"

He shook his head. "I believe she waits for him still. He left during the Borrowed Days, and it's during those days that she returns. For close to fifty-four years."

"Fifty-four years!" It was too romantic. Too much like something a Bronte sister might have written, although this location was perfect for such a tale. I was going to ask what he meant by the borrowed days, but Lachie interrupted, insisting that Angus tell him more stories.

"Aye, that I will," Angus said. "I've one for every day of the year. Now my father, he had two stories for each day. And my gramps could spin tales for weeks at a time without ever repeating himself. You'll want to hear about the Ghosts of Duart. And did ye know, lad, that Mull is the true home of the Witch of Winter? That is not a legend, I swear. It's God's honest truth."

"Just don't scare him too much," I cautioned.

"Dinnae worry, Miss. You leave the lad with me for a wee while. He and I will have our meal in the kitchen, and you can have some time for yourself. Our Miss Proper sometimes perks up a bit when young Americans come to stay. Perhaps you'll be of some help to her. Awa' with you now."

I doubted that Miss Porter wanted anything to do with me, but I needed a break. I would deal with the Witch of Winter, the Ghosts of Duart, and possible nightmares later. I thanked Angus and scurried off to the dining room.

To my chagrin, I had forgotten to make a dinner reservation. Every seat was taken—except for the second chair at a certain table. I beckoned to the host and indicated that I wished to sit across from Miss Porter. He seemed startled, possibly panicked, but he had no choice. He could hardly refuse me the only empty chair on such a grim evening.

Before clearing her throat, Miss Proper gave me a dirty, not-at-all proper look that was almost comical.

"I'm sorry to intrude," I said, "but this is the only available seat. It's pouring rain outside, and I'm hungry, so I'm afraid you'll have to put up with me."

She returned to her curry, and I studied the menu, placing an order as soon as the waiter arrived.

"Aren't you rather young to be taking care of an American pirate cowboy?" she asked quietly after endless minutes of silence.

I choked on my dinner roll. "I'm twenty-one," I said, as soon as I recovered. "Older than I look, but you're right that I've never held a job like this. I thought it would be a great opportunity to see Scotland, but I didn't expect all this wind and rain." I guess I should have considered that it was still March and that this was far north, but all I had thought about was Rory.

"Strange time of year to come," she observed. "You won't see much in this weather. Many Mulleachs come from North America, Australia, and New Zealand, but at more pleasant times."

"Mulleachs?" Sounded like some obscure breed of sheep.

"Natives of Mull. So many scattered during the terrible Clearances. Many of their descendants come back for a visit."

Clearances? Oh, right. That fit right in with my thoughts about sheep. Scottish inhabitants in the Highlands and Western Isles were forced off their land so that the English and Lowland Scots could use the area to raise sheep. It was a cruel act that Highland Scots might never forget or forgive. Lachie's ancestors must have been part of that shameful time, which is why he and his father ended up in the U.S.

"Lachie's father is more than a visitor," I bragged. "He's heading the company of divers that will begin its mission in a few days. You're right about the weather, though. I don't know how they can possibly dive in such awful conditions. Surely it isn't safe."

"Those foolish divers, or at least those that hire them, always stirring up trouble." She stood suddenly. "They'll find no treasure, thanks to early divers who used dynamite." She shrugged. "There probably never was anything anyway, other than a few pots and pans and maybe a cannon. Be careful, Miss America, or you'll find yourself like me, coming back year after year on a hopeless quest. I was your age when I came the first time. And the divers planned to dive then as well, in spite of rain, sleet, and wind." She paused before continuing. "That was also during The Borrowed Days. Always a dreadful time."

"The borrowed days," I repeated. That was the second time I'd heard the expression. When Angus and Miss Porter used it, I could almost hear capital letters. "What does that mean? Why are you here? Why do you keep coming if it's such a bad time?"

She glared at me, a mixture of pain and fury in her eyes, but her voice was soft enough. "Something was borrowed from me, and I would like it returned before I die."

"What do you mean? What did someone take from you?"

She looked at me more kindly, and this time I saw that her eyes were lovely, even as they pinched back bitter tears. "Love," she whispered.

Movie night in the lounge—an old black and white film from 1945—"I Know Where I'm Going," filmed in Mull, the sign in the lobby announced. There were even a few scenes showing the Western Isles, including the dining room where we had just eaten. Evidently, the film was historically important in the life of the hotel and possibly its only claim to fame. A large movie poster hung over the fireplace in the entryway. I thought it sounded boring—I had never heard of any of the actors, long dead—but it was something for Lachie and me to do, something that might keep him from deciding to jump on the beds, which didn't appear sturdy enough to handle it.

Lachie did not want to attend—until Angus Black told him there were scenes of the interior of Duart Castle and, even more interesting, the famous Corryvreckan Whirlpool, located about twenty-two miles southwest from where we were. Angus told me in private that that particular segment of the movie had actually been filmed in a swimming pool in London, but we wouldn't tell Lachie.

"The Corryvreckan is so cool, Francie. It's the third largest whirlpool in the whole world! A lot of boats have been shipwrecked there. I'll bet sea monsters wrecked them." He was prepared to ignore the kissing if it meant even a glimpse of an evil, ancient beast.

We sat together on a couch in the lounge, surrounded by many blue and gray-haired people, including Miss Porter. As for me, I liked the show fine, especially the romantic parts, although I was used to movie stars being more attractive. Like Lachie, I nearly fell asleep until the Corryvreckan woke us up again. My excuse, though, was not the movie. I was tired. Lachie's antics had worn me out.

Later that night in our room, as I drifted off, I heard singing through the wall. A tender sweet voice I recognized, amazingly enough, as belonging to my reluctant dinner companion. I hadn't realized Miss Porter occupied the room next to ours.

> *I know where I'm going*
> *And I know who's going with me*
> *I know who I love*
> *But the dear knows who I'll marry.*

> *Some say he's bad,*
> *But I say he's bonny*
> *Finest of them all*
> *Is my handsome, winsome Johnny.*

The singing was followed by heartbreaking sobs. "Johnny, come back. Please come back, dear."

That's when my opinion of Miss Pauline Proper Porter began to change. She was no longer just a sour, irritating creature, but a tragic one with a story that rivaled the movie we had seen. I would like to know her better, if she'd let me.

More rain the next day, although I did get a message from Rory saying that he hoped to arrive within the week. That pleased me, for I was losing track of the dream, beginning to miss home—wondering if spring had made an appearance back in Iowa. In Bentonsport, the fields would be turning green, buds fulfilling their yearly promise, with streams busy taking inventory of their fish supply, considering the right time to run again. By now, my mother must be planning her garden—"Shall we risk planting squash this year, Martin?"—and complaining about the sudden tightness of her summer clothes, always my father's fault. "How many times have I asked you not to do the wash? You set the dryer too hot." He'd deny it, of course, and they would begin a harmless squabble that would disappear shortly before the next meal when Mom's rich desserts made it clear why her clothes were tight.

And here at this ancient hotel filled with ancient people, I remembered the boys who had taken me to dances and movies and, with the slightest encouragement, would have continued to do so. They weren't a bad bunch. One Gary Stevens could even be a decent compromise. Iowa's winters, of course, were brutal, but spring and summer were perfect. And we never thought about borrowing days or nights, whatever they were.

At breakfast, Lachie insisted that I hear one of Angus's scary stories. "A really creepy one about a laird at Duart Castle who tried to kill his wife by tying her to a rock out at sea."

Fortunately, before he could go on, we overheard a group from the hotel planning an excursion to the museum in town. I must have looked envious, for an elderly man looked in my direction and raised his voice. "You and your little boy are welcome to join us." I pretended not to notice his wife trying to shush him.

First, I informed him, somewhat frostily, Lachie was not my son, and then that we would be grateful to accept the invitation. "Being cooped up in the hotel has been rather hard on him," I said.

Lachie was thrilled at the prospect. "It will be terrific, Francie. They'll have loads of stuff about the Spanish Armada." Even the man's wife smiled at his enthusiasm.

"Yes, I've heard there's a fine exhibit," she said.

The Spanish Armada. That gave me an idea—a way to keep him calm while I finished my meal. As usual, he had gulped his down without much chewing in between swallows. "I don't know much about the Spanish Armada, Lachie." Well, that was true. Other than the gorgeous man who would lead the team of divers, I had no interest in it. "Suppose you tell me about it?"

"Okay. I'll tell you a different ghost story, but Angus says it's true because it happened to one of his cousins. It was so spooky! Wait 'til you hear!"

He was becoming too excited. "Maybe tonight would be better for a ghost story. How about you stick to some basic facts so I'll understand what we're seeing at the museum?"

He sighed before putting on a teacher expression. "I do know all about it. Because of my dad and listening to the divers, of course."

"Of course."

I sipped my coffee and prepared to hear a history lesson from, as it turned out, a rather precocious eight-year-old. It became more than that, though, as our adopted tour group joined in and as I noticed Pauline listening carefully. After those tears, I now thought of her as Pauline. Hearing someone cry kind of makes things personal.

"Well, okay. It all started in 1588 because Spain wanted to take over England," Lachie began. "Spain was mad at England because it helped the Dutch when they were fighting Spain and because England let their pirates attack Spanish ships and take their treasure. The main English pirate was Sir Francis Drake, only they called him a privateer because it sounded more official than pirate. King Philip II was the Spanish guy, and Queen Elizabeth was Queen of England. The old one—not the one today, although I guess she's pretty old, too. King Philip and Queen Elizabeth didn't like each other, which is kinda strange because he wanted to marry her."

"Politics and religion," our host for the museum chimed in. "Always about politics and religion, just like today."

"Right," Lachie said, "but that's the boring part. I don't remember much about it."

The man's wife took over. "King Philip II was Catholic and our Queen was Protestant, of course. That made people enemies back then."

"Even now, sometimes," another woman said.

"Most of the time," someone else chimed in.

Impatiently, Lachie took over. "Spain was a lot more powerful, and it had 130 ships. Everyone thought they were going to win."

The mixed group of English and Scottish tourists began arguing about Mary Queen of Scots and how dreadfully she had been treated by her own cousin. Then one of them wanted to throw Bonnie Prince Charlie and the

Battle of Culloden into the mix, which didn't make any sense. Even I knew that was a different time in history altogether. Soon the refined dining room was filled with a racket seldom heard within those stately walls.

"But the guns, Francie," Lachie yelled, "and the ships. Don't you want to hear about the fighting ships? The galleons and galleasses." He became visibly frustrated as former friends shouted over each other about problems in Ireland and bombs exploding in dustbins off Trafalgar Square.

Then I heard a hoot of laughter coming from a certain secluded table. It didn't seem possible, but I turned just in time to see Pauline dissolved in mirth, behaving like an ordinary person. I grinned at her and was rewarded with a slight wink and a faint smile before she turned away, retreating into herself again.

But I had seen enough to encourage me. Before our time at the Western Isles came to an end, Pauline and I would have a relationship, whether as friend or foe was too soon to tell.

Covered in waterproof raincoats and wearing unsightly boots, we huddled into the mini-van the tour group had rented from a company in Stirling. As if badly needing a plumber, the rain turned on and off haphazardly. One gloomy soul informed us that snow was predicted. "Aye, what you can expect during the borrowed days," was his dour comment.

"The borrowed days," I repeated. "I keep hearing that. What does it mean?"

"You'll not know in your parts," he said. "The borrowed days are the last three days of March and the first three days of April. Topsy-turvy days they'll be. Up and down, never knowing what's what. And folks say you should never borrow nor lend during those times."

"Smart advice at any time," someone said, and the group began a lively discussion about things they had lent, such as screwdrivers and push lawn mowers, never to be seen again. Fortunately, it was a short ride to the small museum at the water's edge.

With the aid of sunshine and warmth, Tobermory surely would be the charming, lovely place you see in postcards and travel brochures. An endorsement of summer—brightly painted shops of red, blue, and yellow reflecting on the water, causing Tobermory to look like two towns. If you gaze hard at the view, then to your far right and up a bit, you'll see a large brown block of a building at the top of a steep hill, called a brae in Scotland. That's the Western Isles Hotel. An easy trek for the hearty in good weather, but in those last days of March, with the waves slapping against the shore and the wind taking unfair advantage, all walks were difficult. The colorful shops appeared old, dull, badly in need of fresh paint. In fact, the entire community seemed clothed in pewter gray. I wondered if I would ever stop feeling damp and chilly. I had read that Tobermory was Gaelic for the Well of Mary, but no one seemed to know why. It is the largest settlement on Mull and was founded in the late 1700s. James Boswell wrote about it when he visited the Highlands with Dr. Johnson. I had thought Mull a weird and unattractive name until I learned it meant rocky promontory or peninsula. Still not an attractive name, but at least it made sense.

Yes, Pauline Porter was correct. It was the wrong time of year to visit, borrowed days or not. I shivered. However, the museum would be a diversion from where I'd prefer being—in front of a fireplace reading a good mystery, far away from Lachie.

"There will be a real Spanish galleon," Lachie informed me. One of the men had been giving him an earful, and I stared daggers at him. He gave me a grin and a shrug.

"Well, maybe a large drawing or model of one," he conceded.

Lachie was not about to be discouraged. His imagination would fill in for the lack of what wasn't there. As it happened, even though the museum was tiny, I found it fascinating. It reminded me of some of our small volunteer-run museums back home, where many of the displays could have been winning entries in middle grade science fairs. For Lachie, the most interesting items were actual treasures retrieved from former dives.

"Look, Francie! Platters and guns and anchors and shields and coins and everything. There's certain to be plenty of gold bullion down there for my dad's divers to find. I hope he gives me some. I wouldn't spend it. I would keep it forever!" Lachie was especially thrilled with a large brass cannon. "Boom!" he cried, to mark the occasion.

To my surprise, I became engrossed in the exhibits showing the early history of Mull—the problems of the Clearances, in which the English conquerors forced the people off the land, the farming, crofting, fishing industry—things I'd never considered before. If I was going to be a writer someday, I needed to broaden my horizons, as Dad had said.

Both Lachie and I pored over the exhibits of Duart Castle, which we would visit when it opened for the season, whether or not the present laird had returned. "Hey, Francie, there's the story Angus told me—all about the lady on Lady's Rock. We'll see it when we go to the castle. Well, not *in* the castle. We'll see it way out in the water, if the weather is okay. The Laird of Duart wanted to murder his wife. He didn't want her anymore because she couldn't have sons. That seems kinda mean, don't you think? Anyway, he tied her to a rock so the waves would drown her. But she got rescued instead, so when he saw her he thought she was a ghost come back to haunt him. She scared him to death. It served him right, even if he was a Maclean."

It was as gory a tale as he had led me to believe. Some of those early lairds were a nasty lot. "Here's your family tree," I said, changing the subject by pointing out a long line of Lachlans and Donalds. "There's the present laird, Sir Lachlan Maclean, and if you could continue drawing the line, you'd see your dad and . . ." I paused, allowing him to work out an imaginary timeline of succession.

"Me! After my dad, Ruari Mor Maclean, would come me, Lachlan Donald Maclean." He frowned. "I don't suppose I'll ever be a Sir."

"No, but you're still plenty important," I said. "And since I'm your teacher now, I must be important, too."

"Oh, you are, Francie. You are very important to me." I received a wide smile, accompanied by a warm hug, and had to admit there was a sweetness about him. If only the weather would clear, and there were things for him to do.

"Time to go, Miss Cummings," our host declared. "We're all fair tired and fancy a cuppa and a biscuit."

They were always fancying a cuppa and a biscuit, I thought, the snarly coffee addict rising above my polite surface. Tea, in my opinion, should be consumed only when one is confined to the sick bed. Time for me to rebel about several things, but I waited until we stepped outside before deciding. Yes, the wind had settled down considerably, and while it was still raining, it was more of a spit than a pour. I might regret it later, but I couldn't go back to that stuffy hotel to spend the afternoon entertaining a small boy.

"I think Lachie and I will check out the town and then walk back," I said cheerily. "I saw a sign saying a boat will take tourists out seal watching today. If it's still scheduled, maybe they'll include us. And if not, we'll get a bite of lunch somewhere."

Lachie cheered with delight, and our new acquaintances looked at us as if I'd suggested a swim to the caves of Staffa or an outing by rowboat to the Corryvrechan whirlpool. We ignored their gasps and comments, gave them pleasant waves of thanks, and made our way to the pier.

"Do you mean it, Francie? Do you really mean it?"

"I mean it—*if* a boat is still going out and *if* they'll take us. Don't get your hopes up too high, Lachie."

Lesson learned. Never tell a child not to get his hopes up, I thought, watching Lachie race ahead of me to the dock. They pay no attention to *ifs*.

Fortunately, the boat trip would take place in a few hours, and because of the many cancellations due to weather predictions, we had no trouble booking passage. It was a trawler and seemed a safer option than a catamaran. At least we could go to the inside cabin if the water was too rough.

"You'll need to do what I say, Lachie," I insisted. "I can't have you blown overboard."

"I wouldn't like that either, Francie. I want to see some real live seals."

"We have time to eat lunch first," I said.

Oddly enough, we saw our first seal as we headed for a restaurant. All we did was look over the wharf and one popped his head from the water, startling us more than it did itself. Lachie was beyond delighted. "Take a picture!" But by the time I'd recovered enough to locate the camera hidden deep inside my purse, the creature had disappeared.

"Never mind," I said. "We're sure to see plenty later. But that was super special, Lachie. You must tell your father about the time you and a seal saw eye to eye."

"And nose to nose!" He was thrilled!

After sandwiches and a quick stop at the Chocolate Shop to load up on snacks for the trip, we returned to the boat launch and were allowed to board early. Soon our trawler, the Turus Mara, was headed for Loch Linnhe, a site that was advertised as seal haven. The captain told us to look carefully for banana-shaped rocks.

Just nonsense to tease a kid, I thought, until we actually saw those rocks against and perched on top of a larger rock. "Black bananas," Lachie yelled, and then the bananas started to move and to dive. "Seals," Lachie breathed— his day complete. This was fortunate because those were the only seals we were to witness. But our boat trip was proclaimed a great success by all aboard. We weren't the only ones suffering from cabin fever. Passengers and crew ended the day on a first-name basis.

By the time we trudged back up the brae to our hotel, it was dark, raining heavily, the wind a howling fury. Lachie dragged his feet, and I had to practically force him as well as myself to keep on going. Dinner would be long over, but I was hoping Angus could rummage up something. Bowls of soup would be perfect. And there he was, right on the other side of the door, seemingly waiting.

"Well, well, I'm that glad to see you," he said. "You have no idea how worried she's been. After me every quarter hour asking if yer back."

"She? Who? You don't mean Miss Porter? Why would she care? Didn't the tour group tell you where we were?"

"Aye, but that wouldn't satisfy the madam."

"We're just fine, and we had a wonderful day."

"Seals," Lachie muttered. "The black bananas were seals."

Then Angus noticed how exhausted Lachie was and after pulling off his boots and helping him out of his wet raincoat, hoisted him over his shoulder. "Off to bed, lad. And you, too, miss. I'll have Nelly send up soup, sandwiches, and a glass of milk." I gave him a pleading look. "Aye, and a cup of strong black coffee," he added.

Nodding gratefully, I followed them up the stairs.

I tackled Pauline at breakfast. After all, Angus said she had been concerned about us. Lachie was sleeping in—a good plan, I thought. This last day of March was miserable: dark gloomy, howling wind, rain. No going out for us today, and I needed to keep him occupied.

Swallowing hard, I took the seat across from Pauline. She peered over her newspaper at me without expression, saying nothing. I had to start.

"Angus said you were worried," I began.

She looked ready to deny it but gave in, shrugging. "It seemed odd that you hadn't returned." Then she looked around anxiously. "Or maybe you haven't completely. Where is the boy?"

"Lachie? Of course he came back, but he's still asleep. All that cold fresh air, getting soaked, and the excitement of seeing live seals have wiped him out." I gazed out the window. "He can sleep as late as he likes. I doubt if we're going anywhere today."

She abandoned the newspaper, poured another cup of tea, adding cream and three lumps of sugar. "The last of March is always the worst of the Borrowed Days," she said, stirring slowly. "If all goes well, tomorrow will see a turn. The first of April normally marks the shift. You should be safe planning for an outing then."

"April Fools' Day back home."

"Which is where?"

"Bentonsport, a small town in Iowa for me. Lachie and his father are from upstate New York."

"Via Scotland, once upon a time," she added. "His mother?"

"She died."

Pauline nodded. "Try the library on the second floor. You'll find books about the Spanish Armada. Some are for children."

I thanked her. "I'd like to find out more about the Tobermory Galleon. Searching for sunken gold. So romantic." Suddenly I remembered a poem I hadn't thought about in years.

I'm the last alive that knows it. All the rest have gone their ways—
Killed, or died, or come to anchor in the old Mulatas Cays,
And I go singing, fiddling, old and starved and in despair,
And I know where all that gold is hid, if I were only there.

Pauline gave a disgusted grunt but also looked at me in surprise. "A verse from *Spanish Waters*. How would you know such a thing?"

I just shrugged. "John Masefield. I read a lot." I continued.

Spanish waters, Spanish waters, you are ringing in my ears,
Like a slow sweet piece of music from the gray forgotten years

Telling tales, and beating tunes, and bringing weary thoughts to me
Of the sandy beach at Muertos, where I would that I could be.

"I used to know the whole thing, but it goes on forever."

"*We anchored at Los Muertos,*" Pauline quoted. "The Isle of Dead Men. Fitting, don't you think?"

"I guess so. It's not about the Spanish Armada, of course, but parts of it could have been."

"I'm surprised you've even heard of it, but the ship you and others persist in calling the Tobermory Galleon was probably the San Juan de Sicilia. If the day were clear, you could look out this window and see the exact spot where it exploded. Sometimes I wonder if this whole island is nothing but a large, improbable ship, adrift in a giant ocean, searching for land, never to reach port." And with those strange, almost poetic words, she took a final sip of tea before leaving the dining room.

Such an odd conversation—neither friendly nor unfriendly, and the fanciful ending decidedly weird. I wanted to ask her where she was from in the States but couldn't muster the nerve. If I did mention it, she would realize Angus had been talking about her. As things were, I thought Pauline would tolerate me at her table as long as I didn't consume too much of her time or become personal. But it was progress, and I had to admit that she intrigued me more than anyone I had ever met.

I finished my breakfast quickly and ordered a tray to take back upstairs. Meanwhile, I came up with a plan for the day, thanks to Pauline Porter.

"Lachie," I said, as soon as he scarfed down his breakfast—eggs, bacon, oatcakes—and gulped his hot chocolate, managing to burn his tongue, "today, we will begin our school."

"Oh, no, Francie. This is our vacation. Besides, I've decided I'm done with school. I really don't care for it."

"You're only eight, silly boy, but okay. You're done with school, but I'm not. So we'll have a different kind of school."

"Different?" At least he seemed intrigued.

"Yes, we'll switch. You'll be the teacher, and I'll be the student."

"Hmmm. What about books and paper and stuff?"

"I've got the paper and stuff, and Miss Porter told me there are books about the Spanish Armada in a library on the second floor. So that's where our school will be today, and our subject will be history—the Spanish Armada. What do you think?"

He put on a solemn expression. "I'm a very strict teacher."

I said I'd take my chances.

The library turned out to be comfortable and undiscovered. At least, no one was there but us. There were several tables with straight-backed chairs, some comfortable armchairs, good lighting, and books, of course, but not too many. I had no trouble finding the ones for children Pauline mentioned.

Fortunately, Lachie was an excellent reader for his age and fascinated by a children's book that told of a ship wrecked off Ireland. "It's very interesting, Francie," he said earnestly. "There was this guy named Thomas de Granvela, who was fighting for Spain and wore a gold ring that belonged to his grandmother. For luck. It had her name and date on it and everything." I smiled at this. Lachie was fond of adding *and everything* or *stuff* to his statements. "Well, this guy Thomas was on two wrecks. but he wasn't killed when the first boat crashed. Then he got put on a galleass called the Girona. That one sank near the Giant's Causeway. Doesn't that sound cool, Francie? Giant's Causeway? Then poor Thomas and lots more drowned. But here's the weird thing. Way back in 1967, divers found the Girona and lots of stuff inside. And can you guess what they found?"

Of course I could, but I didn't want to spoil Lachie's tale. "A large cannon?"

"Well, maybe," Lachie conceded. "But the special thing was the ring! And you could still read what it said inside." He peeked into his book. "It said Madame de Campagney . . . I don't think I said that right . . . 1524!"

I agreed that it was an incredible story. In the next few hours, Lachie worked laboriously, printing vocabulary lists, test questions, and giving me reading assignments, vocabulary lists, and test questions. He didn't realize he was doing most of the work, reading, writing, spelling, and using his clever brain. I took great delight in getting a few answers wrong so that he could scold me indignantly. He was really quite fierce, and I hoped he wasn't mimicking his boarding school teachers, though I feared he might be.

Although I enjoyed the ring story, I didn't find the rest of the subject matter interesting, especially since my teacher felt it necessary for me to identify the types of ammunition on the fighting ships and how to fire a muzzle-loader. But at least I could talk intelligently with Rory if the occasion ever arose. I was working on the first draft of an essay, "Laden with Gold— The Tobermory Treasure Galleon," when Lachie interrupted, holding up a thin, bedraggled collection of children's poetry, written by children.

"Francie, look. It's a funny poem about Sir Francis Drake. I know I've heard it before—somewhere."

I read it quickly. It was awful. "Maybe you just read something similar, Lachie. These poems were self-published by an English schoolteacher years ago. I don't know how you could have found it back home."

Lachie shook his head, puzzled. "I don't either, Francie, but I must have. Sometimes I know things. Sometimes I get confused."

"Readers always do," I comforted him. "We read so much that we often forget where we found it." I didn't share with Lachie my thought that the poem might have been plagiarized by a child managing to fool a teacher.

Lachie announced he was hungry. It had been hours since breakfast. He put the poem behind him, ready to move on to more important concerns.

"Good idea, and I have a surprise up my sleeve. Should be coming about now." As if on cue, there was a knock on the door. In came Angus with a giant pizza, followed by Pauline Porter, carrying a bag of sodas and other goodies.

"May I crash the party?" She asked, smiling uncertainly. "That is the current American expression, isn't it?"

"It is, and you may, absolutely," I said. "And you can see how excited Lachie is." Although it was hard to tell what pleased him more—the visitors or the unexpected lunch treat.

"Pizza? A real live pizza? How did you do that?"

We all laughed. I had found the number of a delivery place in the large folder in our room entitled, "Things to do in Tobermory," and recruited Angus to make the phone call.

"Wow! Pepperoni and sausage and mushrooms and extra cheese! Just like home! Thank you, Angus!"

What followed was a delightful afternoon, once Teacher Lachlan announced that school was over for the day and that I had earned a B-plus.

It must have taken him all of two seconds to determine my grade. He wanted that pizza.

I wouldn't say that Pauline was the life of the party, but she wasn't a wet blanket either. Even though she was older, I detected a bond between her and Angus—almost as if she were leaning on him like a father. Maybe there was a resemblance between him and his father, whom she had known before.

Soon, Angus turned to storytelling, and the more frightening the stories, the more Lachie appeared to enjoy them. I supposed that was normal for a boy. I was growing tired of them, though, and thought Pauline might need lighter fare, too. "Don't you have any funny stories?"

"Aye, lassie, that I do." We settled back again. "It's about the laughing ghost of the Western Isles Hotel. Have ye heard our ghost yet?"

We shook our heads.

"Well, well, you might, although our ghost prefers kinder weather. Come June he's almost rollicking. Pay good attention and listen now." He switched to his storyteller's voice, and we learned that Angus's stories somehow required a great deal of Scottish brogue.

"Once upon a time, many years ago, before my time and my father's, a gentleman from Dundee came tae stay at the Western Isles with a group of friends. As many do, they came for the fishing, and like most fishermen, they enjoyed a good joke—aften about the one that got awa'. Now, this mon from Dundee—ye ken his name was Gordie—had nae sense o' humor. Not a lick. Could never get the handle of a joke or a riddle. Weel, he would join in laughing, but his friends could tell he had nae mind tae the meaning of the thing. Sometimes they would laugh because he didnae get the point, but he was a guid friend and a fine fisherman who always shared his catch, so they liked him jest the same."

"What were some of the jokes, Angus?" Pauline asked, her eyes twinkling. I was happy to see her engaged.

"I don't know for sure, but I can guess. These particular fishermen always preferred a riddle." Angus cleared his throat. "What fish go tae heaven when they die?"

Lachie looked disgusted. "Angelfish, of course. That's too easy."

"Nay, not for Gordie. He thought and thought about that one."

"Let's hear another," I said.

"Very weel. They will be getting harder. Where does a fish keep his money?"

I got that one. "In the river bank," I said.

"Och, yer guid." Angus told us a few more. Why is a fish easy to weigh? Because it has its own scales. Why did the fish blush? Because he saw the boat's bottom. Lachie howled over that.

"Weel, I'll come tae the ending now. One day, the fishermen asked Gordie another riddle—one that perplexed him mightily. Ye see, it was the same one they'd asked him before—Why did the fish blush? Gordie remembered the answer, although he still wasnae certain why it was funny. 'Because he saw the boat's bottom,' he said, that sure of hissel'. But the men shook their heads. Nay, this was a different fish, they insisted. That fish was from the River Nith. This other fish was from Pitlochry. It didn't blush because of a boat's bottom. It had another reason. Gordie thought about this riddle all the day. He thought about it while fishing. He thought about it while cleaning his catch. He thought about it when he fried his fish for dinner. Finally, he shook his head and confessed that he couldnae figure it out. The answer, his friend said, was quite simple. Why did the fish blush? Because the sea weed!

"The answer didnae help Gordie. He didnae understand. And he still didnae understand when he went tae his bed that night. Then right before he fell asleep, it came tae him. The sea weed! How embarrassing! Crikey! The sea weed, right in front of the fish. And Gordie began tae laugh. He laughed sae hard he fell right outa bed and had a heart attack right there on the floor. Then he died upstairs at our Western Isles Hotel. And he died before he could tell his friends he understood the riddle. His ghost is still laughing, and if you chance to hear him, let him know you are that happy he got the joke and that it would be fine if he would jest stop his laughing and rest."

It was a wonderful story, although I wondered if Angus might have made it up on the spot. Many of his tales seemed that way—presented so naturally you would think they had never been told before.

Like Gordie, Lachie didn't get the riddle at first, but he wasn't quite as slow. When it came to him, he was almost as much out of control as Gordie. That's when Angus wisely suggested a laughter and storytelling break to take the garbage remainders of our feast down to the kitchen for disposal.

As soon as they left, Pauline looked through our schoolwork. She chuckled over my attempt to spell *galleas* and my definition of *breech* as a type of trousers rather than the bottom part of a gun barrel. Funnier were Lachie's barely patient corrections.

Pauline smiled at me. "I suspect you're cleverer than you pretend. Do you suppose the teacher or the student learned more?"

I smiled back. "I suspect it was a draw."

"You're not a teacher, are you?"

I shook my head. "I'm not really anything yet. I've only had two years of college. I suppose I'll finish someday."

She looked at me sharply. "Don't wait too long. I did, and by then it was too late. When there was time, the money wasn't there, my family had disowned me, and nothing lay ahead but years of being miserable as an underpaid secretary living in a London slum."

Wow! Quite a revelation from the reclusive Miss Proper! Unfortunately, Angus and Lachie returned, so her true story did not continue. Angus was finishing up a sad, frightening tale about a long-lost lover, who had fallen overboard a mighty schooner and had become a tasty dish for a whale. I shot a warning look at him, but he didn't notice. Without expression, Pauline rose from the chair where she had seemed relaxed and comfortable for once. "Perhaps I'll see you later at dinner," she said primly.

Dismayed, Angus watched her leave. "Och, I cannae believe I did sech a thing," he said.

I *couldnae* believe it either. It was unlike him to be so tactless.

"Finish the story, Angus," Lachie insisted. "Or start from the beginning, so Francie can hear it, too. It's so exciting!"

"Perhaps another time, lad, when we're quite alone. I'd best be getting about my chores now." Clearly, no one was more annoyed with Angus than himself.

And then he was gone, too. "What happened, Francie? Why did they leave?"

Might as well tell him the truth. "I think it was because Angus's story hurt Miss Porter's feelings. Miss Porter had a long-lost love, too. Angus was mad at himself for being so thoughtless."

"Oh." He thought it over. "Did he fall overboard? Is her story scary, too?"

"It could be. We don't know." Yet, I added silently. "I think it's important that we be careful of Miss Porter's feelings."

Lachie nodded. "Because she's the Broken Lady," he said sadly.

Late that afternoon, shortly before dinner, the hotel staff, at wits' end trying to find a way to amuse rained-in guests, showed more films in the lounge. This time, old videos of the children's show Balamory were the offering. I thought the programs were cute, showing animated and live shots of Tobermory, including a train I hoped we might ride one day. The stories were simplistic but fine, although I preferred our own Sesame Street and Mr. Rogers. "Lame, lame, lame," was Lachie's verdict. But it was a restful way to end the day.

That evening another chair had been added to the dining table where one had the finest view of the bay—had it not been dark or raining. Smiling from ear to ear, the host led us to Pauline's table. "We were that surprised. You are the first to be honored in such a way."

Lachie and I were on our best behavior. "Good evening, Miss Porter," I said. "How kind of you to invite us."

She looked sharply at me, as if knowing that while I meant it, my little speech was out of character. "I thought it might be pleasant after our afternoon together," she said. Then she pulled a brochure from her purse and handed it to Lachie. "This is for you, young Master Maclean. If you ever visit London, and I'm sure you will, you must see this replica of Sir Francis Drake's ship, the Golden Hinde. It's on permanent display in Southwark, a short bus ride away from where I live."

"Wow! Cool!" Lachie couldn't have been more genuine American. "Look at the picture, Francie. That was one of his best ships. Drake sailed around the world in it. I think replica means fake. Are you sure it's not the real Golden Hinde, Miss Porter? It looks absolutely authentic."

I blinked at Lachie's knowledge and vocabulary, not that I had known many eight-year-olds to compare him to. Pauline's smile, though, was amazingly kind and sweet. "I'm certain it's an absolutely authentic replica," she said. "Perhaps someday we will tour it together."

Lachie smiled his delight.

"My favorite story about Drake," Pauline said, "was his refusal to confront the Spanish Armada until he had finished his game of bowls."

"Time enough to play the game and thrash the Spaniards afterwards," she and Lachie chanted as one voice.

Pauline definitely approved of Lachie now. I wished I could tell how she felt about me. She seemed to run hot and cold where I was concerned. We enjoyed our meal but remained quiet until she broke the silence again.

"The weather will improve tomorrow," she proclaimed, as if having insider information. "Windy, most likely. You should take your waterproofs, but possibly no rain will come until later in the evening. That will be good news for you."

"Why?" I wondered. "Is something special happening?"

"Indeed there is, and because your teacher did such a good job teaching you today, perhaps he'll give you a break from your studies." She winked at me.

Lachie grinned. "That was pretend. Francie is the real teacher. Besides, tomorrow is Saturday. We won't have school on Saturday. What should we do, Miss Porter?"

Out of her purse came another brochure. "The Isle of Mull Railway will open for the season. You'll want to be among the first passengers to board, of course."

Lachie nodded. "We saw it on that Balamory show. It looked okay."

"I remember seeing signs for it," I said. "It's an N-gauge train that starts near the Craignure ferry terminal, but I'm not sure where it goes."

"Torosay Castle, a fine home. I'm sure you'd enjoy touring it."

"A castle? Can we see it? Francie, I want to take a train ride and see the castle. Can we go? Please?"

"I don't know why not." His father had given me plenty of money for Lachie's entertainment, but because of the weather, hardly any of it had been spent."

Lachie turned to Pauline. "Will you come, too?"

"No, thank you," she said. "But I will have my afternoon tea at Duart Castle, which also opens to visitors tomorrow. I always visit on the first of April."

"Oh," Lachie said. "Maybe we should go there instead." He sounded disappointed. From no choices, suddenly we had too many.

I had been studying the brochure. "There's no reason why we can't do both," I said, while he looked at me hopefully. "We'll take the bus to Craignure, hop on the first train of the day, tour one castle, and then take a bus to the next castle, which happens to be your castle, Mr. Lachlan Maclean. The ancestral home of all Macleans!"

"Yippee!" he shouted in an unlaird-like way, startling the other diners and causing Pauline and me to cover our ears. "Can I wear my new clothes, Francie? Then everyone will know I am a Maclean."

In Oban, I had purchased some needed clothing for him—a Maclean of Duart Tartan windbreaker, scarf, and beret. The Maclean tartan was attractive—red and green blocks with yellow, blue, and black stripes, and I wanted to purchase a scarf for myself. "Oh, no, Francie," he told me seriously. "You must not wear the Maclean tartan. It wouldn't be right." I reached for another, but that was vetoed, too. "The MacDonalds are the Macleans' mortal enemies." Surely not today, I wanted to argue, but I settled on a blue and green Clan Campbell scarf, not knowing at the time I had made the right choice for a member of the Cummings family.

The plans formed quickly. If only I'd known it would turn out to be the day that changed my entire life . . . But that's the ultimate human cry, isn't it? "If I had only known . . ." Well, what if I had? Would I have acted differently? Probably, but I'll never know for sure.

That evening, we were invited to a ceiledh, a type of Scottish party oddly pronounced kaylee. All of the residents of the hotel were invited, and for a small fee some of the visitors staying at bed and breakfasts in town planned to come, in spite of or because of the weather. "Usually there are pipers at ceiledhs," Angus confided, "but there be none available tonight." One of the cooks played the piano, though, and was coaxed into participating. A hat was placed on a nearby table in hopes of a small remuneration.

To my surprise, Pauline Porter joined us, apparently still in the good mood we had found her at dinner. Or perhaps she had never left the dining room, which was where the ceiledh was held.

She obviously loved music. She tapped her feet and sang along, seeming to know all the songs. I knew she had a lovely voice, for I had heard her through our bedroom wall. In fact, "I Know Where I'm Going" was one of the songs sung. I had never heard most of them, other than some of Robert Burns's poems set to music, but enjoyed listening to "The Carlton Weaver," "I Love A Lassie," and the "Flower of Scotland." Some were funny, even slightly naughty. Lachie roared over "Donald Where's Your Troosers?"

Then, to my amazement, Pauline offered up a song. We had just finished singing "If It Wasn't for the Weavers" (If it Wisnae for the Weavers):

> If it wasn't for the weavers, what would we do?
> We wouldn't have cloth made out of wool
> We wouldn't have a coat, neither black nor blue,
> If it wasn't for the work of the weavers.

And, yes, it took me a while to translate all the dialect they sang. Then, after signaling to the pianist to play the song again, Pauline stood next to the piano and announced, "This is in honor of the weather and the wellies we are growing tired of wearing."

> If it wisnae for yer wellies where wid ye be
> You'd be in hospital or infermery
> Cos you would hae a dose o' flu or pleurisy
> If ye didnae hae yer feet in yer wellies.

Wellies turned out to be high waterproof boots made of rubber, and we would become sick of them all too soon. They were named after the Duke of Wellington, who, though not the inventor, instructed that they be made.

Back to Pauline. The famous Scottish folksinger, Andy Stewart, couldn't have had as boisterous a reception. Everyone laughed and cheered. Smiling and blushing, Pauline soon retired for the night. Then the pianist played soft, crooning melodies while a few people sang the words in maudlin fashion. Lachie put his head on the table and fell asleep.

I chatted with Angus about what had occurred. "Lassie, in all the years I've been here, I've never seen the like. You and young Lachie have cast a spell on our Miss Proper."

"I don't think we did anything," I said. "She seems to like Lachie, and a few times today I thought she might even approve of me. I'm as surprised as you." During the afternoon and at dinner I'd had a glimpse of a sense of humor, but now I knew Pauline could be absolutely delightful. How different she might have been if she hadn't been overcome by sorrow.

We ended the evening with a folksong I considered corny. Although I certainly didn't know it then, it would stay in my head and heart forever. It was called, fittingly, "Tobermory Bay," about an exile longing to return to his homeland.

> *I'm yearning for my Hebridean island,*
> *The mountains there are heather sweet today.*
> *It may be just because my heart is Highland*
> *I long for Mull and Tobermory Bay.*
>
> *My dream of Mull grows stronger still and stronger,*
> *So strong it is I dare not disobey.*
> *It's home for me, I can indeed no longer*
> *Resist the call of Tobermory Bay.*

I roused Lachie and got him upstairs to bed. Before he fell asleep, though, he reached up and gave me a hug. "That was fun, Francie," he said. "The best part was Miss Porter's song."

Yes. It definitely was.

I awoke with a start in the middle of the night to the sound of laughter. First from Lachie, and then from I'm not sure who. It was chilling. "Lachie, what's wrong? Why are you laughing?"

"Can't you hear the ghost, Francie? He's so funny you can't help laughing."

I heard but didn't find it funny. "Go back to sleep. We need to be rested tomorrow." Amazingly, he obeyed. But I couldn't sleep, for after the laughter came another sound. This time, someone or something was wailing. It didn't come from the direction of Pauline's room, so I didn't think she was crying again. Great, I thought—a wailing ghost. Should I ask Angus about it? No, I should not! Then I lay awake for a long time, and morning came too soon.

Sporting a mischievous grin, Angus greeted us in the lobby on that fateful day. The grin and a twinkle in his eye gave me a hint of what might be coming. "Lachie," he said, "I have astounding news, lad. This very day, Nessie has been captured! They're holding her at our own Mull Aquarium on the bay. You are the first I have told."

"The Loch Ness Monster? Really? Thank you, Angus! Oh, Francie, let's go see her right now!" He was almost out the door without so much as a jacket before he paused and turned back, frowning. Finally, shaking his head, he said, "The aquarium is awfully small. Nessie can't be comfortable, and she must be so scared. I don't think your news is good at all. What will they do to her? It will be like when the scientists captured ET." Lachie's face crumpled—on the verge of tears. I don't know how they had determined Nessie was female, but I was fairly certain where Angus was going with this.

He grinned delightedly, not really understanding how upset Lachie was. "April Gowk, lad. It's Gowkie Day!"

Lachie was bewildered and unhappy until I set him straight. "Angus must mean April Fools' Day. You've been April fooled, Lachie. They must have a different term for it in Scotland."

"Aye, that we do. A gowk is a cuckoo, a foolish bird, as are all who fall for tall tales these next forty-eight hours."

"April Fools' Day lasts only one day back home. I guess we're lucky. We'd better stay on our toes here. Now settle down, Lachie. Nessie is still safe and undiscovered. Perhaps you and I will go to Inverness someday and search for her. In the meantime, let's figure out a way to trick Angus. Soon it will be his turn to beware." And I gave Angus a look that meant, "Watch yourself, buddy." He smiled happily, accepting the challenge, not understanding that I really meant it.

Lachie returned to his usual self, and you could almost see his mind plotting revenge. He'd trick Angus, he would!

To our surprise, Pauline did not appear at breakfast. I was worried about her, so as soon as we finished eating, I went in search of Angus again. He was in the library tidying magazines and brochures that were already in perfect order.

"Och, you'll never see her at breakfast on the first of April. And when you do later today, you'll hardly recognize her." At my puzzled expression, he sat on a couch and went into storytelling mode. "She will be wearing her finest clothes and fixing her hair neat and proper before she takes her annual journey for afternoon refreshments at the castle. She'll be cheery and hopeful today and maybe still a wee bit tomorrow. Then, on the third of April, the last of the Borrowed Days, she'll be the sad, abandoned soul you first met. The next day after, she'll leave, and we will not see her at the Western Isles for another year."

Fortunately, Lachie had returned to our room, so we could talk privately. "Do you mean . . . ?" I sat next to him but couldn't finish. It was too preposterous.

"Aye, that I do. Every first of April, she expects to see her sweetheart returned to her, as if he never left."

"But it's not possible. She is an intelligent woman. How can she think such a thing? Is she . . . ?"

"A bit of an April Gowk herself? Could be, could be. Aye, once a year she is. As far as I can tell, she thinks March lent her love to April, and April will someday return him to her good as new."

"And she gets all dressed up as if she were young and going on a first date? How pathetic! How incredibly sad! Oh, the poor woman!"

Angus nodded wearily. There was nothing more to say. I left the library and ran upstairs to fetch Lachie and to retrieve my sweater and a raincoat, just in case. We needed to rush to the bus stop, though it looked as if the wind planned for us to go in the opposite direction.

Buses and cars on the Isle of Mull are objects to be avoided. In better weather, bicycles or feet would be safer options. The few roads are so narrow they're no more than paths, at least by our standards. In my opinion, traffic there should only go one way, but that's not how it works. Instead, ever so often there are curved pull-offs on the side of the road called Passing Places. If another vehicle comes along, a game of chicken ensues. Who is closest to the next passing place? Who will be courteous enough to give way or back up or whatever it might take? Usually, if a driver sees a passing place as well as a car in the distance coming toward him, he will pull in, but you can never be quite sure. No one seems to have heard of speed limits, which makes travel even more hairy. And don't get me started on sheep blocking the way! In some respects Mull roads were scarier than ones I'd known on family trips in the Colorado Rockies.

But time is also different on islands. Slower somehow. Sometimes aggravating, sometimes helpful. The slow pace was on our side that day, for the train was delayed, allowing us to board with time to spare.

The Mull Railway was a miniature train with several possible engines. Ours was a blue and red one named Victoria, although Lachie told me it looked exactly like Thomas the Tank. Well, Thomas had been around a while, and I had loved him, too. I also had fond memories of being curled up in my father's lap while he read *The Little Engine that Could,* a book he had saved from his own childhood. I thought Victoria also resembled an engine that might pull cars around a wealthy family's stately Christmas tree or the one at our local mall in Iowa the instant Halloween decorations were packed away. Only two cars were attached to Victoria that opening day since not many travelers were expected. We took seats in an enclosed car with windows, only because of the ceaseless wind. But the ride itself was less than two miles long and other than a few glimpses of the sound, not especially scenic.

I enjoyed Torosay Castle more than Lachie did. It was too refined and elegant for his taste—too complete, done, practically modern. Built in 1858, it was more of a mansion than a castle. As Lachie pointed out, "We've got lots of places back home way older than this." That might not have been true for Iowa, but it certainly was for New York State.

We made short work of touring the big house, as Lachie insisted upon calling it. I enjoyed the paintings—some of them original masters—a bronze head of Sir Winston Churchill, and a library where you could spend a lifetime without ever becoming bored. Outside, Lachie loved the garden statues best, especially the huge lion. Inside, he approved of the model of an Armada ship, the mounted deer heads, and an absolutely gross head of a real tiger that a former occupant, a woman, had shot in India. Both of us declared that our favorite part was the sight from a stone archway—a magnificent view of Duart Castle.

"Let's go there now," Lachie insisted.

"It's not like we can walk or swim," I said. "Let's find out where we can get the bus." But I was anxious to go there, too, and was suddenly excited about the prospect of touring inside. Standing on a cliff top that guarded the Sound of Mull, the castle was spectacular and important. To think that it was Lachie's castle, his ancestral home! I felt a momentary pang of jealousy. I didn't think the Cummings' farmhouse in Bentonsport, Iowa was anything like an ancestral home, even though the Cummings had lived there time out o' mind, as Angus would say.

But Angus had also said something else. He thought my last name might be Scottish, derived from Campbell and Cameron. I had been told my ancestors were French or Flemish, but it seemed, according to Angus, that there was a Willelmus Comyn, who was a chancellor of Scotland back in the eleven hundreds and that I should be able to find information about those early Scottish Comyns at Kelso Abbey. I wondered if Lachie and I could take a trip there when the weather was nicer. Perhaps somewhere I did have an ancestral castle. (Later, I learned that the Campbell castle was Inverrary, a rather famous one. But after what happened, it was doubtful I'd ever visit it.)

And then something simple and avoidable changed the course of my day and, without a doubt, the rest of my life.

We were walking down a grassy slope to the bus stop when I stepped the wrong way into . . . not a hole exactly . . . more like uneven ground, severely twisting my ankle. I grimaced in pain, pausing for a few minutes until I felt I had it under control.

"Stop for a second, Lachie. Let me catch my breath. I'm sure I'll be okay, but we need to go slowly."

He tried so hard to be patient, but he was only a little boy and anxious not to miss the bus. "I'll help you hurry, Francie. Lean on me." With his encouragement and by using his shoulder as a crutch, we were able to go faster, just making it before the bus pulled out for the short trip to the castle.

Once there, I suggested we stop for lunch before touring the rooms, but Lachie was determined to proceed. "Oh, come on, Francie. We had breakfast. Let's just have a big tea today. Please?"

I agreed because it seemed easier than arguing. Also, there was the prospect of joining Pauline for tea and seeing her wearing her finest clothes and being happy—if only for the day. Besides, the pain in my ankle had grown worse, and I could tell it was swelling. I wasn't certain I could endure a bus ride back to Tobermory and needed Pauline's advice on another source of transportation. Perhaps we could share a taxi. If I had only known then how I would return, I would have dragged Lachie back to the bus stop, pain or no pain.

I managed to tour the main floor by dragging my foot, although going up the initial stone steps into the castle was excruciating. We stopped to admire the rowan tree planted right outside the entrance. It's supposed to ward off evil spirits and all who mean harm. I never trusted rowan trees again.

We visited the old-fashioned kitchen and from the Sea Room enjoyed views of the Sound of Mull and Loch Linnhe, where we had gone for seal watching. A sign posted on the wall said that on clear days Ben Nevis, the tallest mountain in Scotland, was visible. Looking out the window, we took the sign's word for it. The Sea Room also offered many treasures. Lachie was pleased to see a small Spanish cannon, an authentic souvenir from the sunken galleon. Then we entered the Great Hall. "Look, Lachie, this is the same room we saw in "I Know Where I'm Going." Other than Corryvrechan, Lachie had pretty much forgotten the movie, but he was impressed by the display of swords over the fireplace. The Great Hall was one of the finest rooms I'd ever seen, and I wished I could remain there for the rest of the day. I plunked myself onto a bench, not just to immerse myself in the room. My ankle was throbbing unbearably.

Lachie did not intend rest for me. "Let's go higher." He gestured toward an odd, skinny turnpike stairway that ran clockwise.

The sign above the stairway was amusing: *We apologize for these stairs. They were built in 1360 to enable one man wielding a sword in this right hand to defend the entrance to the upper keep.*

"Come on, Francie! I want to go all the way to the roof!"

I took a risk. He was awfully young, but the castle seemed safe enough. "I can't, Lachie. I must get off my foot for a while. You go on by yourself, and I'll wait for you right here. Just don't be too long."

He thought it over and seemed to approve the prospect of his own private adventure. He was aware he had received a vote of confidence. "All right, Francie. When I get back, I will tell you everything!"

I smiled. "That will be wonderful." I would sit back and wait patiently.

Lachie kept his word, although when he came back down he wasn't alone. Up on the roof, he'd met some boys on a school outing. He seemed taken with them, and I realized that he must miss comrades his own age, in spite of not liking his boarding school. They seemed a friendly bunch and were well supervised.

"They're going down to the dungeons next," he announced. "Let's go, too, Francie! It will be great!"

I shook my head. I couldn't move. I wasn't sure I could manage to heave myself from the bench in order to shuffle to the tearoom. The school group leader came to my rescue. "Let him come with us, ma'am. As soon as we finish, we're going for a spot of tea ourselves. We'll join you there."

Lachie nodded his head happily, and I couldn't see any reason why it wasn't a good plan. Excitedly, the boys headed down the steep stairs.

There was nothing to do but force myself to my feet and slowly, painfully, holding on to whatever I could, make my way out of the castle and to the small house where the tea room and gift shop were located.

Agonizing minutes later, I took a seat next to Pauline. "Whatever is wrong?" she exclaimed. By that time, I must have looked ready to pass out. Gingerly, I lifted my pants leg, managed to remove my boot, and examined my ankle for the first time. Yes, it was swollen and turning colors.

"Oh, my," she said. "That is nasty. What happened?"

Quickly, I explained. "Just a fluke. I wasn't being careful."

She requested an ice bag. "That will help take down the swelling."

Someone even brought over a small stool so I could elevate my foot. I did feel better, and the tea, sympathy, and raspberry scone with clotted cream helped greatly. Finally, I really looked at Pauline. What a difference!

She wore a soft blue and gray knit dress, perfect colors to highlight her eyes, a silver necklace with matching earrings, and small black leather boots that appeared to be brand new. Her hair was still arranged in a bun, but now it was neat and almost fashionable. The biggest difference was her makeup, well applied, causing her to look years younger—more mid-sixties than seventy-five.

"You look very nice, Pauline," I said—the first time I called her that. I didn't mean to; it just slipped out. She reacted but didn't seem to mind.

"Thank you. This is the one day of the year I try to be presentable, although I'm definitely the April Gowk Fool."

I smiled but didn't comment. I could hardly say that Angus had filled me in on what he knew of her past. My ankle and her attempt to make me more comfortable had broken down some barriers and had also consumed our time and thoughts.

Then she noticed. "Where's Lachie?" Her voice pitched too high made her sound unnecessarily alarmed.

"He found some new friends," I said. "A group of schoolboys, his age and a little older, and their teachers. He met them on the roof, and then they invited him on their big adventure to the dungeons. Lachie did ask my permission." I couldn't read Pauline's expression, but it wasn't encouraging. "He's such a friendly fellow," I added feebly.

"The dungeons," she said flatly. Her face became hard and cold, and I saw the person I had first met when Lachie crashed into her table. "You didn't go with him."

"Well, hardly, not with a sprained or broken ankle!" I didn't mean to sound defensive, but that's the way she made me feel. Guilty. "I was in so much pain it was all I could do to hobble over here. Don't worry. They'll be back soon. The teachers said this would be their next stop."

"Oh." Giving a weak smile, she regained control. "Well, I'm sure it will work out fine. No, I can see you couldn't go down those stairs, and of course he would insist on seeing the dungeons." But something had changed between us. Something significant, and I felt both responsible and irresponsible.

While only a half hour later, it felt like an eternity before the boys and their teachers finally entered the tearoom and made a beeline for the cakes table. I searched for Lachie among them. He was shorter than most of the boys, but still . . . "I don't see him," I said.

Pauline shook her head. She didn't either.

I was able to wave one of the teachers over. "The boy that was with me before? Lachie? He went down into the dungeons with your group. Do you know what happened to him? Are some of the boys still back there?"

The man appeared puzzled. "No, he started out with us, but then we didn't see him again. We figured he had changed his mind and gone back to you." I shook my head. Then the teacher seemed to recall something. "He was talking with one boy in particular. Gene, come here."

A tiny, timid-looking boy joined us. He looked alarmed, as if he were about to be accused of something. "Yes, Mr. James?"

"Buck up, Gene." The tone of his voice was similar to those I'd heard at Lachie's school. "Now, Gene, this lady is wondering where her little boy might be." I didn't bother to clarify the relationship. "Do you know anything? I saw you talking to him on the roof."

"Yes, Mr. James, and we came downstairs, but I don't know what happened next. We started down to the dungeon together, but then he disappeared. I was sorry. I liked him. He was nice to me." Mr. James indicated that Gene should return to the others.

At that point, I wasn't seriously worried. Maybe a bit annoyed by Lachie's disobedience. "He probably saw something that interested him and lost track of time," I said, although I thought it probable that he had grown tired of Gene, who seemed the clingy sort. Then I looked at Pauline. She had stood and was on the verge of panic.

"We must seek help now," she insisted, beseeching the teacher. "The young lady has an injured ankle and can't go searching for the boy. She's his governess, not his parent. "Will you please go back into the castle and alert security? A search for him must begin at once. Especially in the dungeons area."

The teacher nodded, although I'm sure he was looking forward to cake and tea as much as his charges were. He approached the other teacher and talked quickly to him before leaving.

Pauline was definitely more upset than I. "Pauline, don't worry," I said. "I'm sure he's okay. He probably spotted an Armada display and forgot everything else."

She shook her head. "I pray you're right, but I've been in this situation before. I've made a terrible mistake. I never should have decided it was harmless to love Lachie. It's too dangerous for me to love anyone."

What a strange thing to say. Somehow, I knew I couldn't convince her that her fears were unfounded, so I settled back after requesting a cup of coffee. I was absolutely certain Lachie would appear momentarily.

But he didn't. A few security men from the castle came to tell us they had found Lachie's scarf and beret near the Spanish hostage exhibit in the dungeon but no other signs of him. They made a few phone calls and would keep on searching. Then two policemen from Tobermory appeared, followed by two more from Craignure, and then another one from Salen. They asked question after question, repeating themselves often, and I answered everything I could—Lachie's description, the clothes he had been wearing (thank goodness for the distinctive Clan Maclean jacket), the name and whereabouts of his father, their address in the States, my address and background. And, yes, I felt more and more accused and to blame. Was I a suspect? Of what?

Hours passed while the castle and grounds were searched from stem to stern. Closing time came for the tea room, and the last bus would soon be on its way to Tobermory. Pauline was required to leave, and she did so, reluctantly. She glared at the policeman who opened the door for her. "I will see you back at the hotel, Francie," she said firmly. "Soon." She scowled at the policeman.

Finally, the police decided nothing more could be done that night, and a Tobermory policeman drove me back to the Western Isles. He was kind enough but made it quite clear I must not leave the area. Leave? How could I go anywhere—with a swollen ankle and without Lachie? How could I when I was in such pain, physical and mental?

Again, as he had that morning, Angus met me in the lounge—but an entirely different Angus than I had known before. His look of sorrow and dismay could have matched mine. "You'll need much assistance later going to your room," he said quietly, helping me stretch out on the only comfortable sofa in the lobby. I was too distressed to fall asleep, too frightened to cry, or to even care that other guests coming in and out stopped to stare at me. But my whole body demanded rest, and there I would stay as long as possible. Besides, if I stayed, I'd see Lachie sooner when the police found him. Angus patted my shoulder, promising an ice pack and a simple supper. He returned quickly with both those and Pauline.

As soon as we were alone, I turned to her. "Pauline, you knew right away something was wrong. How? And why did you say you should never have loved Lachie?"

She sat next to me and held my hand. "Normally, I'm wrong about almost everything, and I hoped that would be the case this time. But from the first moment I met Lachie, I was worried." She dropped my hand and told me to eat my soup.

I wasn't sure I could. "I don't understand," I said.

"There's no reason you should. I don't understand, myself. Because of his connection with Duart Castle, Lachie's name bothered me. And there was the way I felt myself coming back to life when I met the two of you. And, of course, the Borrowed Days . . . I've been concerned all along. Well, it's past time for you to hear my story, and then we'll pray for a happier ending than mine."

"Go on," I said, although I wasn't certain I wanted to listen. How could it help? A story of the past, when the present one was so urgent? I needed to concentrate on Lachie. But I didn't have the energy to object.

"When I first came to Tobermory with my parents, fifty-four years ago, I met someone—a doctoral candidate from Norwich University, intending to lecture on the Spanish Armada. During the war, he served in the Royal Navy. Afterwards, he went to Spain and journeyed along the entire route the Armada had taken in 1588. He came to Tobermory to do more research and to interview the divers. I was much younger, and I idolized him. I thought he was splendid. In my diary I wrote that he was 'fiercely strong and infinitely gentle.' I laugh at that today, but it was the truth—a combination most women couldn't resist. I surely couldn't. He was seven years older than I with a proud English name, especially fitting for someone who planned to become a history professor—John Rand Burgess. Sometimes I called him my Handsome Winsome Johnny. He called me Pauli."

Pauline

1950

"COME ON, HARVEY, REALLY! ACT your age, not your shoe size!"
"Don't get your knickers in a knot, Angelica."

Pauline winced, pretending not to notice her father giving appreciative whistles to a young woman struggling down the street, skirt blowing all around her. She was having enough trouble hanging on to her packages and swatting down her clothing without putting up with a leering old man. The taxi window was closed, thank goodness. No one else overheard but the driver. Pauline could read the offended outrage on his stiffened back.

At home, her parents had always been somewhat of an embarrassment, but abroad, they had turned into midwestern hillbillies, the low-class bumpkins too many Europeans expected Americans to be. Had they always been this outrageous? They seemed to have worsened since she saw them last. Pauline sighed. How she wished she could have stayed at school in Switzerland. She longed for her life there—her friends, her freedom. Most of all, she missed the kind family that had given her just the right amounts of structure and privacy for the entire time she lived with them.

Pauline had been reluctant, at first, to go to Geneva. She had been shy, withdrawn, without ambition throughout high school. All her life when people posed the dreaded question—"And what do you want to be when you grow up, Pauline dear?"—overwhelmed, she'd be unable to reply. Later in her room, she would think of snappy answers. *I'm considering not growing up* or, perhaps, *healthy and happy* would be a suitable response. But the next time the question was asked, she'd be tongue-tied again.

Then her grandfather, whom she'd never known, died, leaving her mother a great deal of money and large dreams of grandeur. She would spend both. Pauline's parents insisted that she "get her nose out of books and partake of real life." Perhaps they also saw an opportunity to increase their social standing and to finally be rid of her.

"My daughter will attend finishing school in Geneva, Switzerland," she overheard Mother tell her snooty friends. "So cultured and elegant an institution . . . she will come home a fine young lady." What both parents didn't say was that Pauline would be eligible for marriage and no longer their concern.

Switzerland was over, but Pauline didn't feel "finished." Incomplete, unfulfilled was more accurate. After the best two years of her life, she was ready to begin—to start truly living. But under the financial control of her parents, how could that happen? Most likely, she would retreat to reclusive days, content to experience the world through books, considering an occasional trip to the movies with a few girlfriends an exciting event. All meals and social engagements, courtesy of Harvey and Angelica. No doubt they'd line up prospective mates for her to examine—providing Angelica didn't think they were too good looking and as long as Harvey thought their backgrounds were impressive and their portfolios well-padded.

True, her parents had decided to go along with her request to continue her education in the fall. The University of Chicago, if her father could pay her way in; Northwestern, if her mother won, even though Dad insisted it was a school for farmers. Pauline would rather return to Geneva, but whatever happened, it was only late March with the grimmest weather imaginable. She was stuck with nothing to look forward to but six months of feeling worthless, beginning now at the back of beyond.

"Here we are, driver! This is our hotel, the Western Isles. You may pull over now."

"Honestly, Angelica. Do you think he wouldn't know the most prominent hotel in Tobermory? You can't go anywhere without seeing it. Ugly old fortress. Why don't they jazz it up a bit?"

Angelica glared at her husband. "Now who has his knickers in a knot?" Pauline thought she sounded hateful.

"Well, excuse me for living. I just think this whole country needs to step up to the plate. The war has been over for five years, but judging from the tasteless food and the way things and people look—so shabby and old—you'd never know we'd given them all that money. Angelica, we saw bomb craters in London. Bomb craters! You'd think the Blitz was yesterday. They've had five whole years to fill them up and rebuild!"

"Five years isn't a long time when you've suffered greatly," Pauline said softly, more for the driver's benefit than her parents. He must be dying to get rid of them.

They ignored her, of course. Their marital problems, while only annoying before Switzerland, had become unbearable. Dad chatted up any woman in skirts, drawing the line at those wearing pants. Mother flirted outrageously with all attractive men, no matter their age. Pauline wondered if she had gone so far as to having actual affairs. It didn't seem likely, but you never could tell. Probably most of them had too much sense to become involved—unless they found out how much money the foolish woman had. That was a distinct possibility.

Not her concern, she told herself firmly. If she ever fit into their world, she no longer did. But how was she to leave it, and how was she going to endure life until September? How stupid she had been not to plan the next steps—never considering how to support herself. At age twenty-one, still at the total mercy of Mommy and Daddy, she deserved her present situation!

With Pauline's help, the taxi driver removed their luggage—way too much was the opinion projected on his face—and rang the bell for the porter. He shrugged at his paltry tip and zoomed away as if he'd heard that his home had been bombed and looters were on the scene.

"So rude," Mother complained. "I'm glad you didn't give him much, Harvey. I can see why they call the Scotch dour."

"Scots," Pauline muttered. "Scotch is a drink. As I'm sure you'll both quickly discover."

"I had his number right along," Harvey said. "He shouldn't have a driver's license, or maybe they don't require them in this godforsaken country. And will you look at this place? They expect us to stay here? Did you ever see a more forbidding hovel?"

"I think it's picturesque," Pauline said. "The whole town is lovely, even if it is chilly and damp. Do try to be positive. We'll have a good time. Aren't you pleased I've come with you?"

Dad cleared his throat, but Angelica brightened. "It is nice to have you with us again, Pauline. We'll shop and go to fancy teas while Harvey attends his boring meetings. I had forgotten what fun a daughter could be."

And I had forgotten how silly and coarse you are, Pauline reflected. As soon as a likely man comes along, you'll pretend we're not even related. To be seen with her in public and to admit she had a twenty-one-year-old daughter—frightful! People would think Angelica was old!

Harvey beamed. "That's right," he said. "My girls will have grand times. Just don't spend too much of the old man's hard-earned cash, you hear?"

Angelica muttered something about having more money than he, but for once the argument didn't go anywhere.

All would be peachy keen for a while, Pauline decided, and then it would all begin again. Somehow, even in this tiny island community, she had to find a way forward.

The hotel door opened, and Pauline met Mr. Angus Black.

"Our Angus Black's father," I said. At least Pauline's story was diverting my thoughts from both physical pain and Lachie.
"That's right," she said, before continuing.

Later, Pauline wasn't sure why she had taken immediately to Angus Black. Maybe because she had never really known her grandparents, and the old gentleman was her idea of what a grandfather should be. He gave her parents the once-over, polite but dismissive, and then turned to her with understanding. At least, that's what she sensed. "You will be delighted with your room, lassie, especially if the sun ever returns. It's that bright and will wake ye cheerily each morn."

Her mother shuddered. "Not for me, porter. I can't abide light shining on me in the morning. It gives me migraines."

Harvey grimaced. "Well, if you'd stop being a great lump and get up and moving, Angelica, you might not be so bothered."

While her parents continued to glare miserably at each other, Angus gave Pauline a reassuring smile. "I am certain you'll find the rooms to your liking. Ah, here comes the porter, who will show you your rooms on the third floor as soon as you sign the book. I am Angus Black, concierge of the Western Isles. If you find yourself lacking in anything, do let me know."

Pauline smiled an apology at Mr. Black. She suspected he had not been pleased at being mistaken for a lowly porter. In truth, her parents were the lowly Porters, who had no idea they had delivered an insult and wouldn't have cared if they had. Instead—"What? No elevators? Do you expect us to climb those steep stairs?"

"Oh, hush, Angelica. You can't expect all the comforts of home in a place like this. Go along with the man while I sign the register."

There were too many bags for one staff member to handle, so Pauline insisted on helping. "It's no trouble at all," she assured Angus Black. "I'm used to carrying my own suitcase."

"He could make more than one trip, lassie, but that is very kind. Ye will be rewarded by the view out your window."

It seemed to Pauline that Angelica stopped to complain on each step. Her feet hurt, she was hungry but had come down with such a severe headache she doubted she could eat a bite. And the food was certain to be nauseating—grouse, kidneys, and haggis, most likely. "Be careful with that vanity, Pauline. It contains all my cosmetics; I can't have them scattered about. I don't see why that Angus Black person couldn't have helped."

"Mr. Black is the concierge, Mother. He's not a porter; he runs the hotel. It's an important responsibility, and he probably must see to other matters." Pauline's opinion didn't count, of course. It never did.

Pauline took care of the tip, knowing that her mother would not bother with such things. She left Angelica to fuss about her room, one that Pauline found perfectly adequate. Her own room, thankfully, was a distance from her parents'. As a single, it was understandably small, but still comforting and cozy. Immediately, she opened the drapes. Although darkness was upon them, Pauline could see exactly what Angus had meant. From the lights along the harbor, she could tell that the view of the bay was breathtaking—waves crashing high on the shore, tossing the few boats that had not docked for the night, clouds gathered in preparation for another war-like storm that would break soon.

She pulled a small armchair over to the window and sat contentedly. I might be happy here. If I do nothing the entire time but gaze at this view, it might be enough.

A doctor interrupted Pauline's long, sad story. A nasty sprain, he pronounced after examining my ankle, but not a break. He wrapped it tightly and instructed me to stay off of it for a few days. I didn't know how that would be possible, although Angus promised a room for me on the ground floor and offered a hotel wheelchair. The police would return first thing in the morning to ask more questions. Also sometime during the day, Lachie's father planned to arrive with his fiancée. Rory engaged? That figured; all of my plans had come to nothing—not that it made any difference now.

Later, a staff member wheeled me into my new downstairs bedroom. After elevating my foot with many pillows, Pauline sat next to the bed. "Go on," I said. "What happened next?"

"Next," she answered, "the Borrowed Days began."

Day One of the Borrowed Days
March 29, 1950

The next morning, planning to venture down the brae into town alone, Pauline borrowed a Mackintosh raincoat and Wellington boots from one of the maids and grabbed her own umbrella, which would likely turn inside out. Her father, slated to attend all-day meetings, would join them for the evening meal, if he were free.

"Don't bother returning if your lunch is long and wet," Mother said bitingly.

Harvey snarled back. "There you go again, Angelica. Unlike you, I can handle my liquor just fine without your nasty comments." He recovered his false joviality, possibly for Pauline's sake. "Ladies, may you have a rewarding and amusing day." Then he was gone, much to their relief.

Instead of considering what might be rewarding and amusing, Angelica, pleading a headache, opted to stay in bed. "You go have yourself a good breakfast, dear. I'll ring for some tea and toast later, perhaps."

The plan suited Pauline. Time alone would be her goal on this trip: any activity not including her parents. Her breakfast was leisurely, a treat seldom allowed—with plenty of pastries without anyone objecting. The dining room host was the charming, grandfatherly man who had greeted them the evening before. Mr. Angus Black, it seemed, was in charge of much of what happened at the hotel.

After breakfast, Mr. Black gave her a few brochures and some advice on where she might go and what she might do. "Och, not many places open for the season yet," he cautioned, "and a wise decision on the Borrowed Days. Ye might want to come back here for tea at four. We don't always serve, but you'll be in luck today."

Borrowed Days? She wondered what that meant, but Mr. Black had turned to help other patrons. Pauline assured him she would return in time for tea. Probably way before then, she thought, as she faced a bitter wind. By end of day, she would remember that wind as a soft gentle breeze.

Pauline walked briskly from the Mull Aquarium all the way down to the bus station where the town curved around the bay. Inside, she warmed up with a quick cup of tea while leafing through flyers and brochures. Most of what the community offered were outdoor activities requiring decent weather. Definitely she'd like to go seal watching, so she made a note of the times the boats would leave the dock.

"If I were you, I'd also take the trips to Staffa and Iona," said a voice.

Pauline was so engrossed she hardly realized the voice wasn't coming from her own head. "Oh, yes. I've wanted to visit Staffa ever since I heard Mendelsohn's 'Fingal's Cave.'"

"The Hebrides Overture. Magnificent music."

Not her inner voice. She looked up to see a man smiling down at her. A handsome man, not tall but distinguished looking with black hair and dark eyes, wearing a well-tailored suit and carrying over his arm a raincoat similar to hers. Such a nice smile, she wouldn't have been able to resist responding even if she wanted to—which she didn't. It was good to talk with someone pleasant for a change.

Her smile back must have been encouraging, for he sat next to her. "I hope the weather calms down a bit, so a boat trip is possible. I've never been to Staffa, either. In fact, this is my first time on the Isle of Mull." For a second, he seemed lost in thought, as if questioning the truth of his statement.

Had he lost interest in her? "You mentioned Iona," Pauline said nervously. "I saw it on the map, but I don't know anything about it."

He nodded, returning to her. "Another possible cruise, weather permitting. The whole island of Iona is only three miles long but has more history than many small countries. Its original name was Innis nan Dhruidhanean, the Isle of the Druids. It's considered a holy place. According to legend, Saint Columba built the first church there. He is credited for bringing Christianity to Scotland."

"All I know about Saint Columba is that he saw the Loch Ness Monster and ordered it to get lost."

"Right. Supposedly a man about to be devoured by the beast was saved when Saint Columba raised his hand, made the sign of the cross, and cried out, 'In the name of God, you will go no further, and you won't touch that man. Go back at once!'"

Pauline laughed. "And Nessie fled and went to find dinner elsewhere. Funny. I always think of Nessie as being a kindly beast. Do you think it really happened?"

Her new acquaintance shrugged. "Doubtful, but it does make a fine story."

Pauline wanted to ask his name but shyness, as usual, crept in. Reluctantly, she stood. "I'd like to learn more about Iona, but I should go back to my hotel. I skipped lunch and should return for tea."

"Hotel? The Western Isles?"

"Are you staying there, too?"

He shook his head. "Beyond my reach. I'm at Mrs. McGee's guesthouse, not too far from the Western Isles—just up the brae from there. Listen, by the time you make it all the way back, you'll be chilled through. Would you mind if I walked with you? We could have our tea at the Chocolate Shop and continue talking."

Pauline hesitated. She wanted to accept, but would it be proper?

The man smiled. "I assure you that I'm perfectly respectable. My name is John Rand Burgess, and I'm a graduate student of history at the University of Norwich. It doesn't get more respectable or boring than that."

"I'm sure it isn't boring at all. I'm Pauline Porter, and yes, I would enjoy having tea with you." No one at the hotel would give her a thought, except perhaps the concierge. Her mother wouldn't mind; most likely she was still in bed. And the one thing Pauline was sure of—she did not want Angelica to meet John Rand Burgess!

Pauline and John might have had the longest tea in the history of the Chocolate Shop. When they were through, both declared that if either of them had dinner that night, it would be meager and quite late.

She didn't think she had ever felt so comfortable talking with a man, or maybe not even so comfortable with anyone. He was older—twenty-eight to her twenty-one; he had even served in the war, which ended when Pauline was only sixteen. And he was better educated and cultured and, oh, just everything Pauline wasn't! But he found her interesting. She could tell.

He started to laugh. "You herded goats in the Alps? What an incredible experience!"

"Not in Geneva," she explained. "Geneva is a city that takes itself seriously. But my host family took me with them when they visited relatives in Interlaken."

"Gorgeous place. I was there briefly before the war, but I certainly can't match your experience."

The afternoon was like that. They had read and enjoyed many of the same books, listened to the same music, loved certain poets, appreciated the same playwrights. John even suggested that she stay in Britain to complete her education. "Excellent universities in London, of course." Then he smiled. "Or you might consider Norwich."

Would she? Oh my, if only she could remain. It would be better than Switzerland—if John were there. If somehow she could manage not to return to Illinois with her parents . . . But without their financial help . . .

John explained that his undergraduate studies concerned the history of Britain's wars, particularly the one in which he had just fought. "Something happened when I was in the Royal Navy," he said. "Maybe I'll tell you about it one day. Anyway, it caused me to be interested in shipwrecks throughout history, especially those in the Spanish Armada. We touched upon it lightly in school when I was a boy, but nothing at University. I decided to learn more. I'm fairly fluent in Spanish, although I must say the version spoken back then was quite different." He was looking forward to interviewing those backing the divers as well as the divers themselves. "I am at a loss to know why they think anything still remains."

"My father has invested a lot of money," Pauline admitted. "It seems a gamble to me. I hope they know what they're doing."

John nodded soberly. "Indeed, it is a gamble, and I doubt I'd invest, even if I had money to spare. I do understand the lure of treasure, but even if the divers come up with amazing riches, it will be up to a court to decide who gets what. I wonder if the investors know that. The Duke of Argyll has claimed it." John grinned. "He wants more than fancy socks, and the law is on his side. The divers are different; they're experienced and are paid up front. If a treasure remains, they'll find it."

"Why do people think there's something there?" Pauline had never thought much about it before. Her father's business never interested her— until now.

"Well, a ship belonging to the Spanish Armada definitely exploded off Tobermory Bay in 1588. Most people assume it was the fighting ship, the San Juan de Sicilia, although it could have been the Florencia. Supposedly, that ship was carrying the pay of the entire Armada. It might have carried the crown that would be placed on King Phillip's head after Spain won, as was thought to be the certain outcome. As many have learned throughout history, it has never been wise to underestimate England."

"But you said it was the Florencia that had the payroll, not the San Juan de Sicilia."

"Yes, but the rumor is that both ships carried large amounts of gold. Back in 1683, a Scottish diver brought up nine bronze guns, a few anchors, a rudder, and a silver bell. Other things have been found, but nothing of great value. This dive could be different because of better equipment for the divers and more advanced detecting equipment. Some of it is very complicated and difficult to understand."

Still, Pauline wanted him to continue, although she doubted she would comprehend anything terribly scientific. However, the proprietor of the Chocolate Shop announced he would be closing soon. She and John had been there for hours, and tea at the hotel was long over. Reluctantly, they left.

He escorted her all the way up the brae to the hotel. Because of the wind and rain, it was more of a push, shove, and cling than a walk. Soon, they were laughing away their discomfort. There was no point in being embarrassed. As John said, "If we don't hang on to each other, we'll be able to see for ourselves if the waters are hiding Spanish gold."

Too soon they reached the hotel. "This has been grand. I wish we could continue talking somewhere warm and dry, but I have a dinner engagement." Perhaps sensing her disappointment, John went on. "With some people I need to interview." He opened the door. "May I see you again?"

Pauline nodded shyly.

He smiled. "Then I'll call you tomorrow, Pauli."

Tomorrow. Could she possibly wait that long? There were days back in Switzerland she had declared the best in her life, but nothing could hold a candle to this glorious day, unless it might prove to be the next one.

Had she been missed? She had been gone for hours. Angus had noticed John but only smiled knowingly. The old man didn't miss much. That was all right. Pauline liked Angus. He did not judge her by her parents. But John might. They must not meet.

A note on her bed. Did Mother have a key? Not that she had anything in her room to hide—yet—but she was too old to have her privacy ignored. The note was simple enough. Her mother had met some "perfectly charming" people at tea and was now napping. They were to meet her father for dinner, downstairs at eight. Some business associates would join them.

Awfully late for the Porter family to eat. Back home, dinner was at six sharp, the second her father came home from work. And if it weren't ready, he would express loud disapproval. Eight was closer to what Pauline was used to as the dinner hour in Switzerland. Her father was bound to complain about it, but probably later—not in front of "business associates."

As for her, she might never be hungry again—until she could eat again with John. She tried to recall what they'd had for tea but couldn't remember a thing. Did she have hot chocolate or tea? Did she have sandwiches or scones or both? No doubt it was all quite delicious, but all she recalled now were John's dark melting eyes and sweet smile.

Whatever should she do for the next three hours? She was too wound up to nap. She looked through the information portfolio the hotel had provided. A library on the second floor was one of its attractions.

Pauline was delighted to find several books about the Spanish Armada—some written for children. Since she knew so little, it might be a good way to begin. She chose one for adults and two for children. When she saw John again, she would be able to discuss the Armada intelligently. She skimmed through the shortest book. It seemed that back then James, the King of Scots, wanted his countrymen to treat the Spanish sailors humanely and to help them return home. He had ulterior designs, for he was hoping to be named Queen Elizabeth's successor to the throne. What followed was a gory tale that didn't have much to do with the Armada. Perhaps some of the Scots did treat the Spaniards fairly, but that certainly wasn't the case with Lachlan, Laird of Duart Castle. Or perhaps it was the Spaniards who didn't keep their agreement with the laird. Either way, it did not end well.

Pauline tried to figure out an invention used by early divers called a bell jar, but it was too confusing. She'd take the books to her room and try again later.

I choked back sobs remembering our library school. I still had Lachie's assignments to show Rory. I mentioned this to Pauline, and she gave me a strange look. "I'd keep them if I were you. They could prove important." Shrugging, not understanding, I suggested she continue her story.

Pauline took a hot shower and dressed for dinner. For a change, she took time over her hair and makeup. Seeing an older man meant she needed to appear more sophisticated. Her hair blowing all over the place wouldn't do. People often told her she looked like that new actress, Audrey Hepburn, who was going to play Gigi on Broadway. Pauline stood on her bed in order to see all of her in the mirror. Maybe if Audrey were blonde and had blue eyes . . . They did share a certain quality. She would capitalize on the resemblance. She swooped up her honey-colored hair until it balanced precariously on top of her head. Then she outlined her eyes, extending the pencil out a bit, reshaped her eyebrows, and was careful to be discreet about the rest of her makeup. A simple soft knit dress in shades of gold with a deeper gold knit shawl, gold dangly earrings, and mustard-colored suede pumps. There. She was even more glamorous than Audrey!

Pauli, she thought, reveling in the nickname. Pauli Porter. Pauli sounded sophisticated, but what could be more common than Porter? Burgess was much more impressive. Pauline Burgess for formal—Pauli Burgess for everyday. Both were huge improvements over Pauline Porter. Oh, what a pity John couldn't see her now. She supposed she would have to go for something more casual when she saw him again, but she did need to take greater care in her appearance. It was time to join her parents for dinner. And while there, she would think of nothing but John and their wonderful day.

Most of the group had gathered at the table when Pauline made her entrance. Her mother looked her up and down, appalled. Pauline almost shuddered at that dirty look. Did Mother consider her competition? What an absurd thought! Dad, though, was pleased and rushed to pull out her seat. But he nearly tripped, and some of his drink splashed onto the tablecloth, although he managed to grab the glass in time.

"Oops," he said, speech slurred. Pauline's heart sank as she smelled his breath. But she seemed to be the only one bothered by his behavior. Others at the table were in a similar condition, including her mother. That must have been some tea!

Not everyone had arrived; they would wait before ordering, Harvey told a waiter. Then it happened. Three more people walked toward their table, and one of them was John! The very thing she had dreaded!

Her mother perked up immediately. "I'm Angelica," she said. "Do sit here next to me."

John had no choice. "Thank you," he said, but he smiled across the table at Pauline, whose heart was racing too fast to do anything but nod. Angelica noticed the exchange and frowned.

A man seated next to Harvey made the introductions. Fortunately, he stuck to first names. Pauline crossed her fingers. Maybe John wouldn't figure it out.

"This is David and Harvey and Sean and Margaret and Pauline. Angelica has introduced herself already. I'm Frank, and you're . . ."

"John," he said. "John Rand Burgess."

So far so good. John started a conversation with the man next to him about what he expected the divers to find. For the most part, he ignored the woman next to him, Angelica, edging closer to her prey.

Pauline was hopeful until the waiter showed up, and her father destroyed it. "Drinks all around," he said grandly. "More of the same for all of us. Except for my gorgeous daughter, Pauline, of course. Bring her a glass of milk. And my wife, Angelica, seems to have had too much already. She'll have a cup of strong black coffee." Everyone but John, Angelica, and Pauline roared with laughter.

"Absolute nonsense, Harvey. You will have your joke. Bring Pauline the milk, but I'll have the same as John. What are you having, John?"

"A glass of white wine, please," he told the waiter.

Angelica made a face. She loathed white wine. "Perfect," she said.

"I don't drink milk," Pauline said. "Only in tea. Water will be fine, with tea later."

She couldn't very well say that she wasn't comfortable drinking with her parents. Anyway, the damage had been done. Her parents had put her in the nursery, making it clear she was not one of the *real people*. Later, she had no idea what she had eaten—she was frozen in misery. The voices flowed on and on while she sat dazed, barely conscious of hearing anything as the hours passed slowly.

Back in her bedroom, a great weariness swept over her. She could not endure this. Somehow, she would leave Tobermory. Another delightful time with John would not happen. After meeting her parents and seeing how socially inept she truly was, he wouldn't contact her again. It was over. Dropping her dress to the floor, not even taking the pins out of her hair or removing her makeup, Pauline crawled into bed, pulling the covers tightly over her head.

I fell asleep, too, Pauline's voice only a distant drone. The next day was filled with pain, tears, and endless questions and accusations. The accusations came mainly from Rory. How dared I allow a child as young and small as Lachie to go off by himself? Rory never dreamed he had hired someone so negligent. I caught the looks Pauline and Angus gave each other. Why, they agreed with Rory! They understood why I had let him go, but they heartily disapproved. Rory's fiancée Abigail, an alluring sexpot if there ever was one, clung possessively to Rory and gave me threatening looks. Fortunately, the police took the school assignments as evidence that Lachie and I had had a good relationship. Pauline was right about their importance. After dinner, on the second most miserable day of my life, Pauline continued her story.

Day Two of the Borrowed Days
March 30, 1950

Pauline didn't expect John to contact her, but to be safe she had left word at the desk that she was in the dining room. He might call, even though it was past nine already. She had awakened late but less depressed, even somewhat hopeful. Surely he wouldn't hold her parents and that ghastly dinner against her. They and their guests had been the rude ones. She and John had been the exceptions. It was important to think positively for as long as possible. Pauline determined to focus on something else. Mr. Black, approaching her table to wish her a good morning, gave her an idea.

"The borrowed days," she said. "I keep hearing that expression. What does it mean, Mr. Black?"

"Call me Angus," he said, joining her for a cup of tea. "I hear Mr. Black, and I look for my father, God bless his soul. He worked at the Western Isles, too, as will my wee son, only twelve now, when I'm no longer able." He chuckled at her astonished look. "Surprised? Yes, I'm a bit long in the tooth to have such a young'un. After four grown daughters, my bonnie bride and I were taken aback, too. But do call me Angus."

"Angus, then. Thanks. I'm Pauline."

"Well, it might not be considered proper, miss, but I'll try when we're quite alone. Now, to answer your question, the Borrowed Days are an old Scottish legend that may or may not be true, but one must take mind of it. I'm that careful each year. They come during the last three days of March, when it is said that March borrows three days from April. Then, listen, April keeps score and wants those days returned, so she makes haste in taking back the three days. So the legend goes that the Borrowed Days last for six whole days, 29, 30, and 31 of March, and the first through the third of April. Aye, and just the thought will make one shiver, for the weather can be the fiercest of the year. All things, not just snow, rain, and wind, are possible those days, so it is wise to be prepared. And, mind ye, never borrow nor lend anything during the Borrowed Days. Ye'll regret it if you do."

"What an odd legend. How did it start?" Pauline thought he must enjoy telling stories.

"Och, well, my dear Gran told me what happened in the very beginning. It is said that April lent March her most precious and beautiful daughters— flowers, mind you—and dressed them in the loveliest of lavender. April had become weary of naming her flower children, so she called all of this new lot Heather. She trusted March at the time, but never again. March wouldn't return the daughters and so angry he was with April for asking, he raged wind and rain upon them until they blew away forever. Only one was spared, and March saw well that he couldn't care for such a fragile creature. He returned her to April, the mother. April cried bitter tears over her daughter, who was very ill. Suddenly, the poor child's garment turned to the purest white. She was even lovelier than before. April bore many more daughters of violet hue. And her daughter in white grew to have daughters with white clothing, but they were far fewer in number. And that is why white heather is rare in Scotland. Some say it grows only over the final resting place of fairies. It has become a symbol, ye see, of enduring love. So take care, Miss Pauline, never borrow nor lend during the Borrowed Days. Ye'll take the chance that what is taken will no be returned."

"Do you really believe in it, Angus?" It was a charming story but did sound like superstitious nonsense. She wondered if his grandmother had invented it for a particular reason.

"Aye, that I do. Especially on the Day of the Gowk."

"Gowk?"

"The first of April, the day of fools. The early druid priests tried their best to ward away evil spirits, but they still need our help. We must do our part to confuse the spirits so they are not able to do harm."

"Oh, I see." Pauline smiled, suddenly understanding. Another version of their April Fools' Day, although the Scots seemed to take it more seriously.

After assuring Angus she would be cautious and treat the borrowed days with respect, Pauline retreated to her room. It was becoming more and more evident that she wouldn't hear from John, but she would pretend it could still happen.

Pauline spent the rest of the morning staring at the phone in her room. Lunchtime came, but if she went into town, she would miss his call. What call? She must accept that soon her life would revolve around mealtimes. What should she have for breakfast? Should she go out for lunch? Would she join her parents for dinner . . . and would they be sober? John was an aberration. He had never happened. Brushing her hair and letting it fly free, ignoring makeup, she left the room.

Her hand was on the door handle as she prepared to meet the wind, when a girl at the main desk called her back. "Oh, Miss Porter, I almost forgot. There's a message for you."

"What? How long have you had it? Why wasn't I notified?" If only it wasn't too late!

"I am sorry, miss. People kept ringing me up, and I forgot."

There was nothing to do. "It could happen to anyone," Pauline said quietly, suddenly realizing she had sounded as harsh as her mother.

The message was from John. He was sorry for the late notice. He'd been tied up with his interviews. Would she be available for lunch at one?

The clock over the lobby desk proclaimed that it was exactly one. And the front door opened, and there was John.

"Wonderful," he said. "You're right on time."

"John, I just got your message—this minute. I don't think I can go like this . . ."

"Like this? Like what?

"The way I'm dressed, and my hair . . . It's a mess."

"It is, rather. Like yesterday. Real. You're perfect the way you are. I wasn't sure I recognized the Hollywood starlet I was introduced to last night."

Pauline grew hot, embarrassed, but completely happy. He preferred her to the Audrey Hepburn imitation. Fortunately, her raincoat and high wellies were in the downstairs coat closet. Often guests left them there to dry.

"Fasten up your mac now. It's nasty out there. I've made reservations at the Galleon Grill."

Pauline grinned. "That suits both the day and one of your favorite subjects." Reading about the Armada might come in handy after all.

John ordered an enormous seafood and steak platter for them to share. "Eat hearty. I have a surprise that may mean no dinner for us this evening." Then it was his turn to be embarrassed. "I hope I'm not out of line, but there's a boat leaving in about an hour. I thought you might enjoy a bit of seal watching. I was able to hold two seats, with the understanding that I could cancel if you weren't available."

"Oh, I would love that! I've never seen seals outside of a zoo. Thank you!" Pauline was so delighted she stopped pretending to be mature and proper."

John laughed. "That's how I was hoping you'd react. We won't return until late, though. There are simple refreshments on board, but likely this will be our main meal. Do you need to let your parents know that you won't be joining them at the hotel?"

Pauline shook her head. Then she gathered her nerve. "John, about dinner last night. I . . . My parents . . ."

He smiled. "Wasn't it awful? Don't think any more about it. Someday, if I muster the courage, I'll tell you about my family. My parents are no longer alive, but in comparison to what they once were, yours are the epitome of good taste."

"Mine are dreadful. My mother has become an outrageous flirt, and my father whistles at anyone wearing a skirt." She'd admitted that aloud to him? What was she thinking? Worse, what would he think?

John chuckled. "Flirt and skirt? That reminds me of a little verse I heard my landlady reciting after she had been shopping. Evidently, she saw a man behaving much like your father. It goes like this:

The Devil sends the wicked wind
To raise the skirts knee high,
But God is just and sends the dust,
To close the bad man's eye!

Pauline wished she could find the rhyme funny, but it was too close to the truth. "That probably was my father. I wish God would teach him a lesson."

"Never mind, Pauli. Our families' manners or lack of them have nothing to do with us. Now tuck into those sea creatures on your plate. We don't want to miss the boat."

In no way whatsoever did Pauline want to miss the boat.

"Black bananas!" I blurted.

"Pardon?"

"I was thinking of our seal hunting trip. Lachie called the seals black bananas. We had a wonderful time."

Pauline smiled. "A clever description. John and I had a lovely day, too."

No animals anywhere were as darling and clever as the seals on the rocks of Loch Linnhe that day. Their boat captain and tour guide were the most knowledgeable and intelligent to be found in any boat on any day. And John Rand Burgess was definitely the handsomest, kindest, most wonderful, charming . . . in short, the best man in Scotland, Britain, Europe, perhaps the whole world!

"Look, Pauli, a whale!"

"A whale!" Pauline might have missed it if he hadn't pointed in time. Why, John noticed it before the captain did!

John was first to detect an on-coming gale and escorted her inside before the captain ordered everyone in. Even with wind and rain pounding their tiny boat, Pauline sensed that she was safe and was able to enjoy her sweet tea and biscuits.

"Pauli," John began excitedly, after a short conversation with the captain, "Pauli, the captain has shared some grand information with me—if you're up to the challenge. I don't have any interviews tomorrow that can't be stalled."

"What is it, John? Or do you want me to guess? Shall I *mull* it over?" When had she become so witty and clever?

"A guessing game would be amusing, but I won't hold you in suspense. There is a full-day boat excursion planned for tomorrow, fair weather or foul, to visit the Isle of Iona and the caves of Staffa. We would leave early in the morning and not return until late at night. What do you think? Will you go?"

Pauline didn't stop to think. She wasn't experienced at playing games or pretending to be evasive or coy. "Yes! Yes, I'd love to! Thank you, John!"

As it was, they wouldn't return to the Western Isles until very late that night, either. Both were hungry when they docked again in Tobermory. There might still be a few stragglers dining at the hotel, but neither of them wanted to chance encountering Pauline's parents. A pub near the boat landing was open and not crowded. Fish and chips and a few glasses of ale fitted their needs perfectly.

Once seated, Pauline mentioned Angus Black's stories and warnings.

"The borrowed days—that's a new one on me," John said, "and I don't know about that white heather legend. It sounds as if he might have come up with it on the spot."

"Or perhaps his Gram did. Maybe he had done something wrong and that was her way of scolding. He seemed quite serious about it."

"Those grandmothers need to be taken seriously. Mine was a Maclean. Granny Morag Maclean—a frightening old lady at times. Resembled one of your Salem witches. Mum said she used to go into trances and see things that weren't there. I didn't know her well, thank goodness. She might have been responsible for my mother turning out so odd." He gave a great sigh. "Well, I did hear another legend about the white heather from Granny, but she didn't make it up. It's found in many collections."

"Tell me," Pauline insisted. "Then I'll ask Angus if he knows it."

"It's very old. Let me see if I remember. Once upon a time . . ." Pauline grinned . . . "a well-known Celtic bard named Ossian had a beautiful daughter named Malvina. She was engaged to a man named Oscar, who was away at war. One spring day, Malvina saw a poor soul limping across the moor. It was Oscar's messenger, wounded and bleeding. The messenger knelt before her and said that Oscar had been slain, but that before he died, he picked a sprig of purple heather and asked that it be given to Malvina as a token of his love. Malvina took the flower and her tears soon covered it, instantly turning the purple heather white. Later, each time Malvina walked over the moors, whenever she saw a patch of purple heather she began to cry, and, magically, the heather turned white. She prayed that unlike her, good fortune should come to all who found the white heather. Today, the white heather is considered lucky. It is also the flower of brides. The end. What do you think?"

"Two sad legends," Pauline said, "but at least that one wasn't a warning. I guess I prefer it."

John didn't open the hotel door for her until well after eleven. Angus shooed her upstairs. "Such a tempest if your mum sees you," he said. "Get into bed fast, and she'll think ye have been there right along." Pauline felt like Cinderella, with her own fairy godfather.

Then Angus made a discreet exit into the kitchen, allowing John to risk a simple kiss. "I'll see you in a few hours," he said. "Pleasant dreams."

"You, too, Johnny." There. She had been longing to call him that. She was certain to have the sweetest dreams ever.

A note on her bed greeted her again. "Where are you? I'm really quite distraught. This is unacceptable. Wake me in the morning for breakfast, at nine. No, better make that ten." It was signed: Angelica.

"So sorry, Angelica." Pauline was anything but sorry. John was calling for her at six. She wouldn't ignore her mother entirely. She would simply slide another note under her parents' door explaining that she would be away on a boat ride with friends. The plural on the word "friend" might help a little, although she wouldn't count on it. She would face the music later. It would be worth it.

Day Three of the Borrowed Days,
March 31, 1950

Pauline sneaked down to the lobby at 5:30, earnestly hoping no one would be there. To her relief, the lobby was empty, although a few lights were lit, which was comforting, and she could hear signs of life in the kitchen. With luck, she would see John coming up the walk and make a discreet exit to meet him.

At six sharp, he appeared, and she unlocked and opened the door before he had the chance to ring.

"Excellent," he said. "I do like a woman who is punctual."

"And how about well groomed?" Pauline laughed as the wind gave her a less friendly greeting. "Honestly, I feel blown to bits already. By the end of the day, I'm going to be a raggedy mess."

"I don't think that's possible," he said. "Now, let's stay close together and prepare to brave the elements. Courage is needed for what's ahead."

"We may be out of our minds," Pauline agreed. "Awa i' the heid," as Angus would say." Again she felt clever and witty and fun—feelings she had only with John, although she had come close several times in Switzerland.

"It's quite certain we are mad. Let's keep our fingers crossed that the owner of our boat is just as crazy and will carry on."

On that sobering thought, Pauline grew quiet. What would happen if the trip were cancelled? John might not want to do anything else with her. Then she would have no choice but to face the music sooner than expected.

The weather proved too risky for that particular boat, but an alternative route was suggested, plans easily changed. An hour later, they were on the bus for Fionnphort, and an hour after that boarded a ferry that, unlike the small boat in Tobermory, was able to handle whatever waves and wind awaited them. First stop: the Isle of Iona.

Pauline shivered the moment they docked. Iona didn't appeal to her. Perhaps the weather was responsible for her inklings of dread. The flatness of the land and the absence of trees, other than the Yew, gave the wind rights it never would have in more civilized places. She did not share her lack of enthusiasm with John. "No doubt it's beautiful in summer," she said, "but how can anyone stand to live here the rest of the year?"

But John didn't respond. He seemed lost in thought, spookily so, almost as if he were under a spell. She grabbed his arm. "John, where are you?"

He shook his head as if to delete his thoughts. "I'm sorry, Pauli. I know I haven't been here before, but sometimes I seem to know things I shouldn't. You had a question?"

Pauline struggled to continue. She was shaken by John's shift of mood. She had felt invisible, forgotten. "I . . . I was just wondering. Why would anyone live here all year?"

John shrugged. "It's their home. Some have been here for generations. Not many stay year round, though. Those who do are crofters raising cattle and sheep. Probably most of the people who live elsewhere off-season are involved in the tourist trade. You mentioned the Yew tree. It's actually considered sacred. Iona is probably a misspelling of Iova, which means Yew."

Pauline shook her head. "I thought it meant the Isle of Druids."

"Good memory. But that predates Columba. The name was changed later. Look, Pauli, there's Macleans Cross. No matter how hard you try, you can't get away from Macleans in this part of the world. Let's try to visit my grandmother's ancestral home, Duart Castle, someday soon—perhaps tomorrow."

John had returned to being a scholar and historian. He was fascinated with the Abbey and thrilled to be standing on the very spot where Saint Columba, the Irish missionary who brought Christianity to Western Scotland, had once stood. But if it weren't for the pleasure of John's company, Pauline wouldn't wish to stay. Something besides the discomfort caused by the chilly wind alarmed her about the island. She supposed she appreciated the religious significance, although she didn't consider herself especially religious—going with her parents to their local Congregational church when required was the extent of her devotion. She sensed a great violence here— that angry ghosts still walked. It was unlike her to be so fanciful.

After visiting Saint Oran's Chapel, she changed her mind. It wasn't her imagination or the weather. There were spirits here! After all, next to the chapel was an ancient road called the Street of the Dead. Early Scottish kings had insisted on being buried along this route, possibly because it was a western isle, near the setting sun and, thus, associated with death. The tale told about the chapel was that it couldn't be completed until there was a human sacrifice. Saint Oran himself offered to be buried alive. He would be the human sacrifice. The deed was done, but when his grave was opened a few days later, he was found to be very much alive. Oran declared that he had seen Hell but that it wasn't such a terrible place after all. Blasphemy! And he was promptly—and completely this time—put to death.

"So much was destroyed during the Reformation," John said. "All but three of the island's Celtic crosses are gone. There were 360 at one time—a full circle. That would have been a sight worth seeing." Pauline agreed, but she had had enough of this strange place where druids, Celtic gods, and Jesus formed a strange and unsettling trinity.

Back at the Fionnphort dock, they checked to see that their boat trip to Staffa was still scheduled. The weather was worsening, so the captain decided he'd make the decision shortly before the time to leave. "Must see which way the wind is blowing," he teased, although his joke might have been close to the truth.

A ploughman's lunch at a nearby pub would help pass the time nicely. Pauline attempted to say ploughman correctly, and they both dissolved in laughter at John's efforts to teach her. "I give up," she said. "It's somewhere between a cough and a gargle."

"I applaud your efforts at even trying," he said. "I imagine there are many words in your country I couldn't possibly pronounce."

Pauline didn't think so. America's English seemed to obey phonics rules more than England's and Scotland's. "Tell me about Staffa, John. All I know is Mendelssohn's music."

"That's a lot more than most people know. Do you want science or atmosphere?"

Pauline sipped her ale and helped herself to more chips. "Both, if the science isn't too far over my head. Never my best subject. Maybe a little science and a lot of atmosphere. You're the teacher, and I shall be your attentive student."

"I'm no expert. This is just from my reading, mind you. I've never been to Staffa. Well, the word Staffa comes from the Old Norse meaning pillar because of the tremendous basalt columns guarding the caves. Staffa is one of the smallest islands of the Inner Hebrides."

"Then I can't even imagine how wild the Outer Hebrides must be. Is Staffa inhabited?"

"Not for close to a hundred years. The Celts called Fingal's Cave, the subject of Mendelssohn's composition, Uamh-Binn, which means the Cave of Melody."

Pauline sighed. "That's beautiful. I wonder if Mendelssohn knew that before he wrote his music."

"I would guess that he did. Even though the island is in Scotland, the Irish, too, have many stories about it. The ancient name came about because of the eerie sounds one hears inside the caves. The Irish connection is kind of interesting, especially to me since it links up with the Spanish Armada. Both Fingal's Cave and the Giant's Causeway in Northern Ireland were created by the same lava flow and might have formed a bridge between the two sites. This would have happened over sixty million years ago, so we can hardly be certain. The Irish legend goes that the Giant's Causeway and Fingal's Cave were end pieces of a bridge built by the giant, Fionn mad Cumhaill. Fionn built it so he could go to Scotland and fight his rival, the giant Benandonner."

"I wonder who won. But John, you said there was a connection with the Armada. How can that be?"

"Somewhat of a stretch, but still . . . Most of the Armada ships that made it to and around Scotland were shipwrecked off the coasts of Ireland. There were twenty-eight that we know about. The Spanish galleass, Girona, was wrecked on the Giant's Causeway. She struck what is known today as Spaniard's Rock. You and I must see it someday."

You and I, Pauline repeated inwardly. "Will we go inside Fingal's Cave?"

John shook his head. "In this weather? I doubt it. Today I think we'll be lucky to see much of anything. Boats can't go in, so exploring is done only on foot. There are other impressive caves besides Fingal's. We'll need to come back in late spring or summer."

Someday. Maybe for a honeymoon or a family vacation. Look how she was jumping ahead of herself. You would think she wore a ring on her finger. But it wasn't her fault John kept planting seeds of hope. "What else do you know about Staffa?"

"Well, many famous people have admired it, not just Felix Mendelssohn, who was probably the person who made it famous. Wordsworth, Keats, and Tennyson also visited."

Pauline smiled. "Poets. And now the undiscovered Pauline Porter and the soon to be famous expert on the Spanish Armada, John Rand Burgess, will take their turn."

"You write the poems, Pauli, and I'll write the tomes. We'll be famous, my girl. Whoops! We'd better be off, or the boat won't give us that chance."

Walking back hours later, no longer night but not quite morning, either, after countless jokes and laughter and earnest discussions about whether or not the trip to Iona or the caves of Staffa were more enjoyable, John insisted on an answer. "You must decide, Pauli. Which was your favorite? Iona or Staffa?"

Pauline blushed. "It was Staffa, John. You must know that." Seeing that the wind and rain were too violent once they reached Staffa to do anything more than to huddle in a private corner in the cabin with their lips firmly on each other's, it was an answer that bode well for the future.

John smiled. "That is what I hoped you would say. Someday, Pauli, we shall see the basalt caves in clear, warm weather. And perhaps we'll aim for another rainy day when we return to Iona. We'll reverse things, in order to be fair, of course."

Someday, Pauli thought. There were to be many somedays for them.

Then both of them halted, as if they had suddenly encountered a chill—or an omen. "What is it, Pauli? Why did you stop?"

"You did, too, John. Why?"

Pauline wasn't sure she could explain and wanted to hear what he had to say first.

"I'm not sure. I had the strangest sensation—a darkness crept over me—as if something unpleasant were going to happen."

To her dismay, Pauline's eyes welled up. "The same thing happened to me. A black cloud that said something was coming that would change everything."

"We're being fanciful." John shrugged, attempting to dismiss it. "Tired and overly-saturated with the ancient gloomy stories we heard today." He gave her a quick hug. "And you must admit that not seeing the Staffa caves was exhausting."

Pauline tried to shake off the feeling. Her self-doubts and apprehensions that John was too good to be true and that she didn't deserve him must have entered into it. "You're right—only our imaginations." The tears vanished, but she was still shaking when they reached the Western Isles.

Outside, they stood staring at the hotel, uncertain of what might follow. Finally, "I don't want you to go inside," John said.

"I don't want to go, either." She thought she knew what he meant, but . . . "What do you have in mind, John?"

"The same thing I've had in mind since we first met. You—only you. My landlady and her family are out of town, so I have the house to myself. Come home with me tonight."

"Tonight is over. It's morning now, even if the sun doesn't know it yet." She put her hand in his and gave her parents the briefest of thoughts. No matter. She was an adult and fully capable of making her own decisions.

Later, wrapped in John's arms, she reflected that no matter what happened in the days ahead, she would always have this, and it would be more than enough. Less than twenty-four hours later and for countless years to come, she realized what a foolish notion that had been.

Day Four of the Borrowed Days
April 1, 1950

Pauline awoke, alone in a single bed that suddenly seemed too roomy, too spacious. "John?" Perhaps he was in the bathroom. No sounds, though. "Johnny," she called out again. Then she noticed a piece of paper, the only item on the weathered dresser. Dismayed to find she was wearing nothing, she scrambled to retrieve what appeared to be a message from John and jumped back under the covers.

"Pauli, I forgot about my interviews scheduled for this morning. Try to meet me at Duart Castle at one this afternoon. The bus from the station goes directly there; you'll have no trouble. I hope you won't have difficulties back at the hotel and that we'll tour the castle, have a fine tea, and the rest of the night together. I love you." It was signed, "Your April Gowk."

"Yikes," she cried, pulling on her clothes. If she rushed back to the hotel, she might manage to change, have a quick breakfast, and be long gone before her mother stirred. She recalled that her father was to leave yesterday for meetings in Edinburgh that might last as long as a week. It wouldn't matter if she arrived at the castle early. She'd take a book along.

Angus gave her a pointed, almost accusatory look at breakfast, but he was too much of a gentleman to say anything. She could have imagined his disapproval. After all, she had showered and changed into fresh clothing, and he might not know she had been snug in a man's bed all night and not in her room at the Western Isles. This was so out of character for her, she was having trouble believing it herself. But she shivered in delight. She had worried about sex for years, but it seemed so natural and right with John. Natural, but still the most exciting thing she had ever experienced.

Odd that excitement never destroyed her appetite. She was determined to keep breakfast simple, but everything tempted, and she ended up ordering a full Scottish breakfast: eggs, sausage, buttered toast, black pudding, tattie scones, and several cups of milky tea with three scoops of sugar. Passing by her table, Angus smiled approvingly. He expected people to do justice to the cook's meals. He had little use for those like Pauline's mother, who seemed to subsist on black coffee, whisky, and aspirin.

Pauline wouldn't risk going back upstairs. Most likely, Angelica would stay asleep for hours, but why take a chance? She would freshen her makeup in the downstairs powder room, and then bundle up once more in a sweater and Macintosh. She couldn't endure the unattractive wellies today. My, her belt was tight. The exercise to the bus station, despite the high wind and constant drizzle, would prove beneficial.

She walked against the wind the entire length of the bay, reciting a poem memorized for a high school poetry concert back home. Poetry concerts used to be popular; she wondered if they still were.

> *I must go down to the seas again, to the lonely sea and the sky,*
> *And all I ask is a tall ship and a star to steer her by;*
> *And the wheel's kick and the wind's song and the white sail's shaking,*
> *And a grey mist on the sea's face, and a grey dawn breaking.*
>
> *I must go down to the seas again, for the call of the running tide*
> *Is a wild call and a clear call that may not be denied;*

And all I ask is a windy day with the white clouds flying,
And the flung spray and the blown spume, and the seagulls crying.

I must go down to the seas again, to the vagrant gypsy life,
To the gull's way and the whale's way where the wind's like a whetted
*   knife;*
And all I ask is a merry yarn from a laughing fellow-rover,
And quiet sleep and a sweet dream when the long trick's over.

A sudden blast of wind that almost knocked her off her feet only made her laugh. Well, John Masefield, I've got my windy day, even though the white clouds aren't doing much flying and can scarcely be called white. And the spray is certainly flunging, or should that be flinging? She didn't suppose the seagulls ever stopped their crying. I'm a gypsy, she decided, as she stepped onto the bus. A gypsy wild and free, and soon I'll hear another merry yarn from another John—my John—my laughing fellow rover. Tonight, there will be a less than quiet sleep in his arms, but the dreams will definitely be sweet. That she had misinterpreted the end of the poem didn't occur to her until much later.

The tea room of Duart Castle was busy, even though it was just past eleven. Elevenses. Wasn't that an English expression that meant it was time for a cup of tea? Pauline giggled. Any time in this part of the world seemed to be the right time for a cuppa. Perhaps they had nineses and tenses as well. As tempting as the shortbread, oatcakes, and raisin scones looked, she would ignore them until teatime with John, around four, she imagined. Lunch wasn't part of their plan. But no lunch? She was too hungry; she couldn't possibly wait until four. She made her way to the refreshment table and selected a piece of shortbread with chocolate icing, a small round of oatcake, and a currant bun. No sugar or cream in her tea, she decided virtuously, before adding a splash and three lumps of sugar. This definitely means no lunch, she told herself firmly. With her treats, a book of poetry from the hotel, and a purchased souvenir booklet of the castle, she settled into a corner table that had a grand view of Duart and the sound. Here, no doubt, John would be sure to spot her when he arrived.

To her joy, she found a poem about Staffa in the small book of poetry. She had checked how she had done with the Masefield poem and was letter perfect. And here was a poem by John Keats, yet another John. Surely that would impress her John. She knew in her heart that she didn't need to impress him, but she couldn't help wanting to.

> *Not Aladdin magian* (Was that misspelled?)
> *Ever such a work began;*
> *Not the wizard of the Dee*
> *Ever such a dream could see;*
> *Not St. John, in Patmos' Isle,*
> *In the passion of his toil,*
> *When he saw the churches seven,*
> *Golden aisl'd, built up in heaven,*
> *Gaz'd at such a rugged wonder.*

The poem was much longer, and Pauline found it incomprehensible. She tried to memorize bits of it, but it was hard to memorize something you didn't understand. Maybe John would explain it. Perhaps it was something they could enjoy together.

The specified time arrived, but no John. Then 1:30, 2:00, and then 2:30. His interviews must be running late. Pauline understood. It couldn't be helped, but how much longer would he be? She couldn't possibly consume more sweets or tea, and the woman who ran the tea room had begun to throw questioning looks her way. Others were coming along who might enjoy sitting at this table where she had remained far too long. Pauline stood to leave when a teenage boy dashed into the room.

"Are you Miss Pauline Porter?"

"Yes." At last!

"I'm sorry I couldn't get away earlier to hand this to you."

Of course. A note from John. All would be well soon.

"The gentleman apologized for the delay, but someone was waiting for him in the dungeons." The boy looked around the room. "That was over an hour ago. I'm surprised he hasn't arrived by now." He shrugged, tipping his cap. "It surely will sort itself out, ma'am." Then, somewhat uncomfortably, he rushed out.

The time was 2:45. Pauline opened the note. "Pauli, please excuse the delay. I just learned that I am to interview someone inside the castle. It shouldn't take more than a quarter hour. Wait for me, dearest. John."

But he never came, and she couldn't stay there. As if in a solitary cloud, she drifted over to the castle. At the entrance, she asked everyone she encountered—tourists and staff—if they had noticed a dark handsome man of medium height. Obviously more description was needed. If only she had a photo. She couldn't even say what he had been wearing—probably a suit for interviews. People were polite but shook their heads. Inside the castle she found that she could not proceed until she paid the fee. It was agony standing in the long line, waiting to be allowed entrance. Success, finally! She clamored down the treacherous steeple stairs, shouting frantically all the way. "John! John, where are you?"

The castle guides and guards were alarmed. Some rushed down after her, and others below rushed up to meet her. "May we help, Miss?"

Fighting tears, Pauline showed them John's note. "He's a graduate student, interviewing people about the Spanish Armada. We were supposed to meet at one." It was after three. She had left the bus hours before. The early morning note and this one were the only words she'd had from John all day.

The guards and guides had, of course, seen many men answering John's description, but they hadn't been paying attention or looking for anyone in particular. True, the staff was kind, but they also didn't want any commotion alarming the paying visitors, so they quietly helped Pauline search the castle and grounds—without finding the smallest sign of John Rand Burgess. They promised to call the Western Isles Hotel and speak with the concierge, Angus Black, if they discovered anything.

There was nothing Pauline could do but return to Tobermory. She sobbed during the entire bus ride, causing looks of both irritation and compassion from the other passengers, although no offers of help. Should she be frightened or angry? Was John in danger, or had he forgotten about her? Perhaps he had left deliberately.

Before going to the hotel, she stopped at John's boarding house and rang the doorbell. No answer. The door was locked, and the house, even from outside, wore a sad, empty look.

Angelica wasn't in her bedroom or in the dining room and hadn't left a note. Pauline knew she shouldn't be surprised. Since meeting John, she had ignored her parents completely. Ashamed, she had to admit she hadn't even considered their feelings.

She found Angus ordering staff around in the kitchen. She must find a way of remaining calm. "Angus, do you know of my mother's plans for this evening?" Angus gave her a sharp look as if to let her know she was not fooling him. While he didn't like the Porters, Angus believed that one's parents deserved respect.

Muttering to the dinner servers about being careful not to break any glasses, he opened the ledger on the desk. The Porters had a nine o'clock dinner reservation. "I can't say where they might be now. I believe they planned on visiting a distillery today. Do you wish to join their party? It's for five."

She shook her head and began to tremble. Her father's business trip plans must have changed, but the thought of dinner or any kind of party was unbearable.

Angus led her to a lounge sofa and sat comfortingly next to her. He patted her hand. "Lassie, something is troubling ye greatly. I will help if I'm able."

Kindness. That's what she needed. As soon as she finished spilling out both tears and story, Angus escorted her to the police station. "Let's put it into their hands. They'll sort it out."

While sympathetic, the police could not help. After all, John was a grown man, so he could not be considered a missing person. They must wait forty-eight hours, and so forth. There had been a severe automobile accident outside of town, and all of their officers—all four—were needed. "Foolish people, failing to heed the passing places," one officer declared. "Dinnae worry, miss. You'll hear from your young man. Come back in a few days if he doesnae show himself."

At nine, Pauline went to the dining room. "Well, Pauline," Angelica said coldly, "I see you've finally decided to join us."

"I need your help, Mother," she said simply.

"I've been available for the past few days," she said, turning to a dinner guest.

"Dad?"

"Well, hi there," he said jovially. "This here is my wayward daughter. Pauline, this is," and with slurred speech, he rattled off their names.

"Mother, I need to talk with you in private. Something has happened."

"I'll go to your room later, Pauline. As you can see, we're eating dinner now."

Shaking her head, in tears, Pauline returned to her bedroom and waited for a mother who never came.

Francie

2004

I NEEDED A BREAK. PAULINE did, too. Saying she would fetch tea and coffee, she left the room. I wondered if she felt sheepish about confiding in me. So now I knew that both Lachie and John had disappeared from Duart Castle. There must be a reasonable explanation. Some old castles had deep wells. Could both have fallen, plunging to their deaths? I would ask someone—not Pauline. Concentrating, I managed to hobble to the toilet but didn't make it back before she returned with refreshments that interested only her. After scolding me for not waiting, she helped me into bed and handed me a cup of coffee.

"Go on," I said, mainly to stop her fussing. "What happened next?"

She shook her head. "The Borrowed Days continued; they didn't get any better. The police repeated that John was a grown man. He couldn't be declared a missing person for forty-eight hours."

"Like in the States," I said.

"Well, I was a basket case, but I returned to the castle to search again, anyway. The staff at the castle showed sympathy, not just because they felt sorry for me. They didn't want a bad light cast on the castle's reputation. A solution was important to everyone involved, so they initiated another search and finally, in one of the dungeons, found a handkerchief embroidered with John's initials."

"The dungeons," I said softly. "No wonder you were distressed when you heard where Lachie was."

"The dungeons," Pauline agreed. "Even the word has an evil, cruel sound."

After forty-eight hours, when he still hadn't appeared, the police inquired at the home where John had been staying. "I had returned several times before to check," Pauline said, "but the owner hadn't returned." Finally, the police took his disappearance seriously when Mrs. McGee showed them John's suitcase and, seemingly, whatever clothing he wasn't wearing, as well as his notebooks and books. "I told them his briefcase wasn't there, but I couldn't be sure of anything else. The police had enough evidence to satisfy them. Officially, he was a missing person."

"At least missing children today are considered an emergency," I said, hoping that would work in Lachie's favor.

"They contacted his brother and sisters in Norwich," Pauline continued, "but no one had heard anything from him in months. His friends and professors at University didn't have information, either." She began to cry, although they were old tears, shed often. "Other than being scared to death for John, the worst thing for me was my parents. They showed no heart, no love. How dare I stay out with a man all night? How dare I frighten them so?"

I didn't say anything, but I kind of sympathized with them. I could imagine how terrified my own mother and father would have been if we had been on vacation, and I failed to show up one night. But my relationship with them was different, and I wouldn't have required such secrecy. They might have been displeased, but they never would have turned against me.

Perhaps Pauline guessed what I was thinking. "I suppose I should have left a message. But the odd thing was I think what bothered my mother most was that John had chosen me, not her."

Jealousy. From what she had told me of her mother, I concluded this was indeed possible.

"My greatest comfort was Angus, the father of our present Angus." And other than Pauline, the 2004 version of Angus was my comfort, too—my anchor, my port in this terrible storm.

After a few more days, Pauline and her mother returned home while Mr. Porter stayed in Scotland to take care of his financial affairs.

"At home I couldn't focus. I could do little but cry. I was certain John hadn't left me willingly. He loved me—I know he did. That night he said we would be married, that he didn't want us to be apart ever again. In my heart, I knew John must be in danger or . . . dead."

I looked at an old woman telling me her story as if it had happened yesterday—as if she were still twenty-one. Outwardly she was seventy-five, but inside, at that moment, the fifty-four years had never passed, and her grief was present and strong.

"Then about a month later," Pauline continued, "I learned I was pregnant."

I gasped. "You had a child?"

"I had a dead child—a still-born. And I no longer had parents. Either they disowned me, or I disowned them. It seemed to have been a mutual decision."

"Pauline, I am so sorry." It was hard to know what else to say. "What did you do then?"

"I stayed with my aunt while waiting for the baby to be born—John's baby. It was a little girl. I would have named her Jenny—Jenny Miranda Burgess. She would have had John's surname even without him in our lives. Everything for me would have been different had she lived. I remained with my aunt until I recovered physically, and then I found a job as a secretary. It was difficult, but I counted every penny until I could go to London, where I thought I would find work. I never went back to the States or talked to my parents again."

I remembered the first real conversation I had had with Pauline—the time she had told me about the borrowed days. "Something was taken from me," she had said. "Something I want returned before I die." When I asked her what had been taken, she answered, "Love." Now I understood. Unless Pauline's parents had been quite different when she was a child, and I doubted it, John was the only person who had ever truly loved her. The borrowed days had taken away love.

"I love you," I whispered, as she was leaving the room. I think she heard.

Angus brought in my evening meal and said that Pauline was in her usual spot in the dining room. She had gone back to her old ways, he said. But I knew that it must be even worse for her now. The disappearance of Lachie had to be added to her sorrows.

As for me, all of the unhappiness I've experienced during my entire life couldn't compare to what I felt back then. My ankle didn't matter, nor did the accusatory looks of the policemen, or the dashed pipe dreams about the engaged, enraged Rory. Not even Pauline's fifty-four-year-old tragic love story was important. The disappearance of a grown man with a wallet so many years ago was nothing against a vanished eight-year-old child with no resources at all. The only thing I cared about was Lachie. "Where are you?" I whispered, before I finally drifted into a painful, troubled sleep.

Lachie

2004

LACHIE HESITATED. THERE HE WAS in his own castle having a wonderful time while poor Francie was miserable. Probably he should tell her they could return to the Western Isles and tour the castle another day. That would be the fair thing. But there wasn't much to do at the hotel, and he had waited so long to see his ancestral home, which sounded important and mysterious. Besides, if the weather kept on being bad, maybe they wouldn't be able to come back for a long time. He shrugged, trying to come up with more excuses justifying doing what he wanted. He and Francie would have a fine tea afterward. That would make it all right. She'd be okay again soon.

He liked Francie. She was almost as good as a mom. Much better than that Abigail Dad talked about marrying. Dad thought Abigail was beautiful. Lachie supposed she was, but Francie was pretty, too, although she didn't have enough curves to please Dad. Lachie couldn't figure out why curves were important. He preferred a straight up and down look in girls. That way they looked more like boys.

Speaking of straight up, Lachie was far up now—on the roof, looking out to the sea and the faraway mountains. He was pleased to join a group of schoolboys. Most of them were friendly and the teachers seemed nice, too. He wouldn't change places with any of them, though. Boarding schools were awful. You'd never catch him in one again. The first day he had been so homesick he started to cry. The other boys, even the one in charge, called him crybaby, and every time they saw him, they would go, "Waaaaaaa, there's the baby! Do you need your nappie changed, baby?" He didn't have any friends and was too unhappy to do well with his schoolwork. The teachers seemed to think he wasn't trying hard enough. Finally, he summoned the courage to tell his father what was wrong, and Dad sent Francie to rescue him. Without her, he might still be at that horrible place! Francie. Maybe he should go back. Maybe she needed rescuing now.

Then he noticed a couple of boys picking on a little guy. It appeared this school was just like his—full of mean bullies. The boy tried to get away, but they kept towering over him and making noises like pigs. Lachie to the rescue! At last he would get his revenge. He was ashamed he had never fought back. He was older now—almost nine. This time would be different.

"Hello, there," he said, much to the boy's and the bullies' surprise. "Are these jerks bothering you?" The boy shook his head no, but Lachie could tell it was a big fat lie because he was so scared. The bullies looked as if they planned to switch their meanness to him, so Lachie acted fast, going into an *I'm important* Scottish mode. Standing straight and tall, he tried a Scottish brogue, although not successfully. "My name is Lachlan Maclean," he told them, "and Duart Castle is my ancestral home. Ye'll notice I'm wearing the tartan of my Clan Maclean. Macleans don't like bullies picking on little guys. Sometimes we lock them in our dungeons. And, mind ye, our swords are sharp."

The boys backed off—perhaps because of Lachie's antics, but more likely because a teacher was heading their way. "Sorry, didn't mean anything," one said.

Lachie turned to the victim. "What's your name?"

"Gene," the boy replied.

"Let's be friends, Gene. How old are you?"

"Seven." Gene was even younger than Lachie when he'd entered Webster Academy.

Yes, boarding schools were frightful places. He needed to convince Dad that Francie should stay, even if he didn't marry her. Francie was a fun teacher, especially when she pretended that he was the one teaching. Thanks to Lachie, she almost knew as much as he about the Spanish Armada.

He peered out over the balustrade at the waters beyond. A good spot for his ancestors to notice if any invaders were coming by sea. "Good vantage point," he said, trying out a word he'd learned recently. He confided that his ancestors had owned and controlled Duart Castle since the year 1174. He wasn't certain the date was exactly correct, but he'd read it somewhere, and it sure sounded good. He also told Gene that his name was the same as the present laird's. "Sir Lachlan Maclean, only I don't have a Sir before my name." At least, not yet, he added silently. And he vowed never to tie his wife to a rock or do any other bad things. He pointed out the rock but gave Gene a simple version of the story so as not to frighten him.

"Wind picking up," one of the teachers shouted, interrupting Lachie's boastful storytelling. "I don't want any of you to end up in the channel."

"Well, maybe not some of you," the other teacher said, and the boys laughed good-naturedly.

Before following the group, Lachie looked at the view once again. Then he rubbed his eyes. He could swear he saw a ship in the distance. It looked almost like the model he and Francie had seen in the museum—one of the galleons, a front-liner fighter. But this one didn't seem to be in good shape. It was tattered as if it had been in many battles. He grabbed Gene's arm. "See that?"

"What?"

Lachie pointed. "A ship, way out there!"

"Ah, yer daft," Gene said, jokingly. "Let's go before we're blown all the way to your ghost ship."

Gene didn't see it, so Lachie let it drop. Besides, he wasn't sure what he saw. He looked back, and the ship seemed to shimmer and fade. He shrugged. It happened sometimes. He saw things or heard things or knew things he shouldn't. Meanwhile, he was keeping Gene waiting.

On the way to the display rooms, Lachie explained that Duart meant "Black Point" in Gaelic. "Dubh Ard," he said, showing off. He had practiced saying it over and over until he was pretty sure he got the pronunciation right. "Maclean means Son of Gillean. Gillean of Battle-Axe was a terrible fierce warrior."

"How did they get Maclean out of that?" Gene gave a great sigh.

Lachie didn't know, and he could tell Gene had grown tired of listening to him. After all, Gene was only seven—not almost nine like him. "Oh, there's Francie," he said.

Francie gave him permission to continue with the teachers and students down the steps to the dungeons. It was very nice of her, considering that she was still in pain. Lachie looked back as they left the Great Hall. Suddenly he felt funny, like he was making a huge mistake. Did he just feel bad she couldn't come, too? Well, that might have been part of it, but he doubted she cared much about seeing the dungeons. Something else was wrong. He had a prickly feeling, different from anything he had ever experienced. He almost turned back, but Gene said, "Come on, let's go! It's going to be brilliant!"

Lachie had seen pictures of the dungeon display. He knew that inside one of the cells were wax models of the Spanish officers held hostage by Sir Lachlan Mor Maclean when the galleon was sheltered in Tobermory Bay— before it exploded, of course. But he never expected the models to look so real. The wax looked exactly like skin. He turned to Gene to remark on this, but Gene had disappeared. "Gene, where are you?" None of the other boys or teachers were there, either. That was strange. Maybe there was another dungeon he hadn't noticed. Or maybe they decided to go to the room that had a display of The Swan, a shipwreck that occurred later. Well, never mind them. Lachie was here now, and he wanted to see this awesome display first. Then he'd find the others.

"It's terrific," he whispered, when one of the *men* moved. And then another spoke. It sounded kind of like Spanish. "How do they do that?" A tape recorder he couldn't see? Then one of the figures reached through the bars and grabbed him. "Hey!" Lachie sprang back. That was almost too real— like something you might find in Disneyworld at Halloween time. No, it was too creepy being here alone. He would look for Gene.

But he couldn't. This time, the wax hostage grabbed his Clan Maclean jacket and held him tightly against the bars, practically strangling him. Disney effect or not, this was definitely not funny. "Help," he managed to croak, although not loudly enough for anyone to hear.

Steps rushing down the stairs encouraged him. Oh, good. Gene must be coming. Releasing him, the man stepped back, as if his hostility had never happened.

"I'm here," Lachie gasped, before catching his breath. Then, "I'm here, Gene!"

But it wasn't Gene. Instead, it was a different boy, who resembled Lachie, in spite of wearing old-fashioned clothes, like maybe Scots wore a long time ago. He must have been hired to show people around. The automated models and the dungeons and people in costume did make everything seem more authentic. Lachie looked back at the figures that were giving him dirty looks.

"Ye maun leave at once," the strange boy said. "Ye hae nae right tae be here. These cells are for our captured hostages—unless ye fancy becoming one, yersel'."

He'd had enough. Treating a Maclean like that! "Okay, I'm going. But I have just as much right to be here as you. Maybe more. My teacher paid the admission fee." There. The boy would know he was not alone.

But he shook his head. "I dinnae ken who ye are, but if the laird is tae find ye, mocking the tartan of Clan Maclean by wearing those insulting garments, ye'll likely find yersel' behind bars wit the Spaniards. Ye'll learn they are not a friendly lot."

Lachie had already discovered that. He found the boy a little hard to understand since he spoke with a stronger brogue than Angus and other Scots he had heard in Tobermory.

"The laird would be happy to meet me," Lachie said. "We're sort of related, and we have the same name. I'm Lachlan Donald Maclean. So there!"

"That is not likely, but ye maun come wi' me until we sort this out." The boy pulled Lachie down a narrow hall and to a side door Lachie hadn't seen before. It was old, creaky, and evidently heavy, for the boy had to push hard to open it. Then they were outside.

And everything was different. The air was warm, the grass was green, and Lachie could see flowers in bloom, although they didn't look as if they'd last much longer. The leaves on the trees were colored for fall. Nature had just played the biggest, most impossible April Fools' Day trick on him. Angus's Loch Ness Monster prank was kid stuff compared to this.

As unlikely as his surroundings were, what was true was the reality of the boy standing next to him. He was definitely skin, blood, and bones—not a wax figure. "Who are you?" Lachie demanded, wondering whether to be indignant or scared. Bravery worked before; he would try it again. He had stood up for Gene against the bullies, and now he must defend himself.

The boy examined him carefully before speaking. "We might be kin at that. I am Donald Hector Og Maclean, and if it weren't for your curious clothing and speech and curious way of wearing your hair, we could be taken for brothers. But we'd best save our chatter for later."

Lachie looked back at the castle, and then across the bay. Just barely visible, as if it were in a strange cloud all to itself, he saw the Spanish Galleon he'd seen from the roof. Going back to Francie wasn't possible, but neither was going forward.

Donald took his arm. "I mean ye nae harm, Lachlan Maclean. Aye, ye are dressed strangely, and I can't tell from your speech where ye might be from. But there's another odd one on board. Ye may be of help tae each other. 'Tis certain he needs the help, and it is certain that I owe him."

Lachie nodded slowly, thought briefly of Francie still waiting for him, and followed Donald Maclean.

Francie

2004

"YES, DAD. YES, YOU HEARD me correctly. No, it's not a good connection. What? Yes, I'll be home the end of next week. No, not a word. The police haven't found anything, and Mr. Maclean thinks it's best for me to leave, now that I've been cleared of suspicion. I know, Dad. Yes, it's been very unpleasant. We'll catch up soon. Tell Mom I'll find a job in town this summer and sign up for fall classes at the university. We'll figure it out. I know, Dad. Love you, too."

I hoped my parents would never find out how suspicious the police and others had been of me. Some still were. At times I was certain of arrest, but there was no real evidence. Angus Black and Pauline were my only true defenders. Others staying at the hotel reported on how out of control Lachie had been the evening we arrived. They no longer recalled how cute and endearing they found him later. I considered them traitors. The angry, accusing looks I had received were mortifying—as if they thought I had finally tired of Lachie and killed and stashed him away somewhere. Murdered. It seemed a definite possibility that someone else had done just that.

Shaking, I ended the call with Dad. I didn't want to leave Tobermory with everything unresolved, but I could hardly remain with Rory so angry and, well, mean to me. It was hard to blame him. After all, he didn't know if his son were alive or dead—safe or trapped somewhere. He didn't know if Lachie had left willingly or had been forced or tricked. And, although it was horrible for me, he didn't have anyone else to blame.

I had accepted Pauline's invitation to stay at her flat in London for a few days. We might be of comfort to each other. Then I would go home where I belonged. My parents were worried about me, and I was worried about me, too. Lachie must be dead, and I must learn to deal with it and get on with my life, even if I never forgave myself.

Pauline

2004

PAULINE PACKED HER MEAGER BELONGINGS that now seemed pathetic—clothing, unattractive and out of style—this tweed skirt must be forty years old. She hadn't cared for it when it was new. Where did she buy it? Hutchinson's on Regent Street? That London shop closed twenty-five years ago. No matter, she'd donate everything to Oxfam and ask Francie to go shopping with her for new clothes.

Now for the books. A few favorites—the poetry and the beloved *Heidi* and *Little Women* from her childhood—were put to one side. The rest she would donate to the second-floor library. She would also leave the ugly wellies and the yellow mac. Let someone else who ventured here during the borrowed days have a turn at hating them. When or if she returned, it would be in bright sunshine.

She would take along her diary, although she wasn't certain she'd ever open it again. Definitely left behind would be the invisible item that should never have been packed in the first place. She would leave Hope, for she no longer required it.

Hope was gone. At least the hope of finding John. Starting now and for the rest of her life, hope would be spelled with a lower-case letter and not be a noun but a verb, concerning more immediate and possible things. She hoped that Francie would find some peace with her in London. She hoped that Francie would successfully resume her life back in Iowa. She hoped she would see Francie again. Yes, hope was a verb.

Poor Francie—dangerously close to being charged with kidnapping and, possibly, murder. But there had been no solid evidence and, of course, no body. The police were able to contact some of the people who were on the museum and seal hunting excursions. They remembered Lachie and vouched for Francie's kindness toward him. As it turned out, Pauline and Angus were her best character witnesses. Unless Lachie returned, Pauline doubted that his father would ever stop blaming Francie. Pauline shrugged. It wasn't fair, of course. Not really Francie's fault, she was just young, but the poor man had lost so much—first his wife and now his son. If he couldn't blame Francie, he would have to blame himself. That, Pauline believed, he couldn't bear.

She had discussed this at length with dear Angus. Neither of them thought much of Mr. Maclean's intended. "Aye, if she had been here when the lad disappeared, she would have been the likely suspect." Pauline agreed. The relief on Abigail's face that she might not inherit a stepson was palpable.

Angus. Pauline would miss him. Over the years, both he and his father had been true friends. Angus was the reason she might return someday, without hoping to see anyone but him.

What else would be safe to hope for? She hoped the vegetables would be in abundant supply at the greengrocer. Another hope, but one that might be classified as big—Pauline hoped she would change, becoming more the kind of person she should have been, one who would reach out to her neighbors and not be viewed as unapproachable. She knew that many in the hotel called her Miss Proper. She wondered if people in London did also.

Suitcase closed, and as soon as the maid did up her room in the morning, there would be no sign that Pauline Porter had ever stayed in this inexpensive, single bedroom on the third floor of the Western Isles Hotel. It was time to meet Francie for their last dinner at the table Pauline had claimed for so many years.

There was an absence of joy in Francie, Pauline thought worriedly. A complete lack of spirit, as if she had nothing to look forward to. In so many ways, Francie was responsible for bringing her back to life. She must repay Francie by getting her out of her funk, as understandable as it was.

"Tell me about your home in Iowa, Francie."

Listlessly, the younger woman looked up from the soup she had been stirring mindlessly until it was certainly cold. "You don't really want to know," her expression said clearly.

"Really, Francie. I'm interested. Perhaps I'll visit you there someday." Not likely, but anything to engage Francie's mind.

"Well, we have a farm right outside of Bentonsport, a village on the Des Moines River. Old by Iowa standards—incorporated in the 1840s. It even has a historical district, with a beautiful truss bridge. Not much for young people to do, of course. I couldn't wait to get out, but now . . ."

"I understand," Pauline said. "I felt the same way about my hometown." Except for the last part, of course. There was no *but now . . .* for her. She would never return. "Is it a large village?"

"No. Maybe about a thousand; you pretty much know everyone." Francie seemed to warm up. "I still have friends from high school and a few cousins I'm close to."

"And your parents?"

"Mom and Dad are great." As if recalling Harvey and Angelica, Francie said quickly, "I know I'm lucky in a lot of ways, Pauline, it's just that Lachie . . ."

"I know," Pauline said. She knew too well, and she also knew she would do whatever it took to keep Francie from following in her footsteps. There must be no more borrowed days for her friend. "Will you return to university?"

"Probably, although not until fall. I received my associate degree at Indian Hills Community—it's just a junior college—but I should get my bachelor's. I didn't think I wanted to, but I'm changing my mind."

Pauline nodded. "Not going has been a regret of mine," she said.

Dessert came, but Francie shook her head. "Dad offered to come over and take me back with him, but it would be a waste of money when things are tight already. And I don't want him to see me like this. I'm hoping to cheer up a bit in London."

"That's what I hope. Let me tell you about where I live." Pauline would concentrate on what she liked about London. Certainly, there must be some things. She needed to stay positive—for both their sakes—to keep their thoughts far away from Lachie and John.

"As you may know, I live in Wandsworth, next to Southwark, not the trendiest part of town but such an improvement over when I first arrived in 1953." Heavens, had she really lived there that long? "As I told you, I moved to London as soon as I thought I had my head about me and had saved up enough money to be without a secretarial position for a few months. I was attractive enough to find something without much trouble." She shuddered, remembering how important personal appearance was back then and what women had to endure just to keep their jobs. "I stayed in the same position with the same boss for many years, until both of us retired. You might say we grew old together."

"Was he nice?" Francie asked, coming out of her stupor somewhat.

"Most of the time. It helped that I was the fastest typist to be had and that no one matched my stenographic and shorthand skills. And Robert, that was his name, was interested in me." To the tune of a marriage proposal every six months for close to ten years—until he finally gave up and married someone else.

"But you didn't care for him?"

Pauline shook her head. "Not in that way." No one had ever filled her heart as John had. She felt rather foolish now in not allowing something to develop with Robert when she had the chance, rather than believing that returning any man's affection would make her disloyal to John. She wouldn't mention John to Francie ever again, or talk about the yearly trips to Tobermory. The point was to take Francie's mind off the sorrows of the past and today.

She ordered tea with cream and three lumps of sugar while Francie nursed her strong black coffee. Soon they must leave the table and face the long, melancholy night ahead. The hotel was giving a party, but she was certain neither of them could endure it. Perhaps they would visit for a while in Francie's downstairs bedroom.

"And you've lived in the same flat all that time?"

Pauline welcomed the question. "I have indeed, although by London standards it's considered an attached house. I find it easier to say flat than to explain. It's in a little square called Minnow Walk, where the neighborhood cats would live in constant ecstasy, if there were any real minnows to be had."

"Cats? Do you have any?"

"No, I've never had so much as a goldfish. But I always pet the resident felines when I make my daily walk to our corner newsagent."

"I'll enjoy that," Francie said. "My mother has four cats. It will be good to see them again."

She was starting to look ahead, Pauline thought. This was definite progress. And, Pauline realized suddenly, so was she. Her house, her routines, her teakettle and biscuits, and daily trips that often included bus rides into the West End.

"Perhaps you and I will take in a play or musical," she suggested.

"That would be nice." Francie finished her coffee. "I think I'll go to my room now. I'd like to spend some time alone."

Pauline nodded. "I'll come see you later—just to check in. How odd to think this is our last night here." Her last night after so many nights. If she ever returned, she would insist on a different room. She was saying goodbye to John at long last. But had the years been totally wasted? Probably—it was hard to tell. What she would never regret, though, was a single minute she had spent with John.

John

1588

John Rand Burgess—that was his name. He was certain now—and equally so that he was out of his mind. No other explanation made sense. For hours or days he had lain on this dirty plank floor in an impossible world of intolerable pain—skull pounding, sometimes replaced by dull, intermittent throbs—and voices. Gruff, angry voices speaking Spanish! No, he was crazy. Again, he lost consciousness, for days or weeks.

"My name is John Burgess," he might have said aloud to a scarecrow wearing what looked like a doublet and hose—an extraordinary outfit of tights and a shabby red tunic with bedraggled white ruffles and frayed cuffs. A joke. He was at a party where someone had spiked the drinks. Was he in costume, too? He looked down at threadbare rags. Must be short of cash again if this was what he could afford. "Where . . . ?" he tried to say, but the scarecrow swore something unintelligible before giving him a sharp kick.

Alone again in this dark empty place. I am John Burgess. But who is that? Where is he from? Why is he here? Hurts too much to think. John rested his head on a tattered, oily blanket and remained for weeks or months or years.

It *was* Spanish! A group of swarthy ruffians with strange accents were discussing someone named Medina. He didn't know all the words but understood many of them. He, John, understood Spanish. Could he be in Spain? Was he a Spaniard? He didn't think so. Surely the name John Rand Burgess wasn't Spanish. But the name Medina was familiar. Not anyone he'd ever met, but perhaps read about—once upon a time. Somewhere, but where?

The men were arguing furiously. *Que te folle un pez!* one shouted nastily, warranting a stiff punch that knocked him to the floor. None of them paid attention to John. Certainly they knew he was there. He must not pose a threat or be the cause of their anger.

"Medina would not allow us to quit," another said.

"That is true. He would insist we keep on going as long as one soldier and one lifeboat remain."

"Easy for him to say, assuming he's still alive." The foul-mouthed Spaniard had returned to the fray.

"No more traitorous talk, if you value your life. Philip is King, Medina is Captain, and God is on our side."

The war, John thought. I'm on my ship, back in the war. I must have been wounded. But why are they speaking Spanish? Our king is George VI, and isn't the war over? Yes. I returned to University. London? Liverpool? No, it was Norwich. I'm John Rand Burgess of Norwich, England. I will hold on to that, no matter what.

"Wake up, ye vile Sassenach. We need tae talk."

John stirred. Not Spanish this time. English with a Scottish brogue, and the speaker was young. He raised himself on one elbow. "Who are you?"

"Och, yer back, I see. Well, well, I wasn't sure you'd make it. I'm Donald. Donald Maclean. I don't know why you're here, or where or when you belong."

"Maclean." That was familiar. "My grandmother was a Maclean," he said at last. "Morag Jean Maclean. Strange woman. Always saw things that weren't there." Could that be what had happened to him? Was he delusional, too?

Donald nodded. "Aye, probably a wee bit fey, as is my Granny Morag. Larking with spirits, sending me on daft missions, even to when I don't belong."

"You mean where you don't belong."

"I know well what I mean. I go to when I don't belong, and I know things I shouldn't."

I know things I shouldn't. John had said those words before, but to whom? He couldn't remember. "Why . . .?" He wasn't sure how to finish the sentence.

Donald shrugged. "Why are you here? Maybe you've come to help." Shaking his head, he looked John over. "I hae ma doots ye can even help yersel'."

John struggled to stabilize himself—first his body, then his mind, and then his whole world that had changed into someplace completely foreign. The dull faraway pain was back and soon agony would return full force, taking charge. If only the boy would go away, he would try to sleep. No! Bad idea! There had to be answers. "Where am I?"

"On the wee bit left of the failed Spanish Armada, mate. The glorious San Juan de Sicilia. Nae sae grand now."

The Spanish Armada. 1588. Why did he remember that? "The ship?" John struggled to stand but a wave of nausea nearly felled him.

Donald grabbed his arm. "Not so fast, kin of Maclean. Nowhere for you to go. Mind that you're a prisoner in the hold, about to be joined by more, may my foolish laird of an uncle rot in Hell for his evil doings!"

Oh, his head! "Christ! Give me a bloody aspirin, will you? Oh, never mind," he answered Donald's puzzled look. "That was a wicked blast. Someone help me!" No longer able to think, John collapsed again on his pile of rags.

He was awakened by screams—not from humans this time, but terrified beasts. Then he heard men sobbing, followed by sounds of retching and the putrid fumes of vomit. He could make out just enough Spanish garble to figure out what had happened. In order to save on food and water, the horses had been thrown overboard. The sounds were their neighing screams. Wouldn't it have been kinder and made more sense to kill them and eat the horsemeat? But he wasn't in a position to give advice and was grateful for a sudden electrical storm, causing loud claps of thunder to drown out the pitiful cries.

During the days or weeks ahead, John was aware of people coming and going, speaking gibberish that occasionally became intelligible as English or Spanish. Shadows of figures in ancient costumes drifted by. A young fellow John seemed to recall from another time forced wine down his throat. He wasn't kind exactly but was trying to help.

"Don't ye die on me, Maclean," John heard him say. "You must be here for a purpose, although I dinnae ken what it might be."

John *dinnae* know either. And he *dinnae* care. His name wasn't Maclean. Just leave him in peace—whether to live or die didn't much matter.

Gradually, he was able to stand without becoming dizzy. Stretching hurt, but he made himself do it anyway, experimenting with arms, legs, and knees. Everything seemed to work. Cautiously he crept, exploring his dark surroundings. He was alone. Stairs. He climbed them, at last finding himself on the deck of a once-great ship. Wild land in the distance, possibly an island—might the horses have made it there?—and at the end of a promontory a formidable stone castle. Shouldn't stay. Might be noticed. But he was so hungry.

Stealthily, he opened door after door until he found the galley. Abandoned. Any food? A loaf of stale bread would do. Voices coming closer. He shoved the loaf under his scratchy tunic and dragged himself back down to the hold, where he gathered more rags to pile onto his thin blanket. Something was wrapped in one of the cloths. Hard. A book? He'd examine it later. Tearing into the bread, hoping not to break his teeth, he made a tentative plan. First, he'd make a pillow—he needed to rest, to gather strength. Then, he must try to use his mind again. He lay down his head. It was time to remember.

"You match the description of the gent I was to look for. Is your name John Burgess?" He recalled that young male voice, although he did not know its identity. John had admitted to the name. A mistake, perhaps. The messenger, innocent or traitorous devil, gave him a note. What did it say? Where was he when he was given it?

His memory was returning, although great chunks were missing. He reached for a tin cup of water someone seemed to have provided. The note. What did it say? He was to go to the dungeon of the castle. That's right. Duart Castle—to meet with an expert on the Armada. But John was the expert— a student of history. Why had he obeyed the writer? The envelope included a ticket to the castle. Without an ounce of misgivings, he'd dashed down the curving staircase to the cells below to where Spanish officers once were held while the laird waited to be paid for his generosity.

He had expected to see an exhibit of those hostages—wax images—but the cells were empty and the doors open, and the supposed expert wasn't there. Then what happened? What next? Finally, he remembered! A bag thrust over his head, a foul smell, evil laughter, and nothing else for a long, long time. He came to in the hold of this ship, where he drifted in and out, nauseous much of the time, head throbbing unbearably. He shuddered. A probable concussion—truly a regrettable wonder that he survived. But at least he was remembering. There was something else . . . someone else. A name that just escaped him. An important name. No, not yet. Too tired. One more sip of water, then sleep. Think later.

Angry, scared voices awakened him. Snarling, shrill ones, both Spanish and Scottish brogue vied to pull John away from blessed sleep. A hostage exchange seemed to be in the works as Spaniards exited while bewildered Scots took their place.

"Awa'n bile yer head, ye dobbers!"

"Donald? What's going on?"

"Never you mind," Donald snarled at him before addressing his kinsmen. "You lot won't stay here. Ye'll find better quarters for Macleans." Then he glanced back at John. "If you see this one wandering about, leave him be. He may sound foreign, but his granny was a Maclean with the gift. Don't touch him. But mind the filthy guards, though they are apt to fear you as well."

The men nodded, and John was alone again. In spite of Donald's assurance, he decided to keep his wanderings to a minimum. Someone had either left behind or left for him a crusty loaf and a tin cup of wine. A few bites, a sip, and then a brisk walk around his prison would be the order of the day. And then—a look at his discovery, the book!

The Sea Journal
31 October 1588

I've called the notebook I found "The Sea Journal," although I'm uncertain whether we're at sea or on another body of water altogether. The distant coastline is similar to my memories of the Sound of Mull—the peninsula vaguely the same. And the castle I'm seeing down the coast is surely Duart, although a more primitive version of when I was there in 1950. That is, I think I was there. At times my mind is a maze of confusion. I have no idea how long we have been here, stuck in this one spot.

Another reason for the title is, I suppose, a combination of arrogance and hope. Arrogance that someone will read my writing and decide that I'm a latter-day Jonathan Swift or Daniel Defoe; also hope that I'll return triumphantly to my own time, with a journal to prove what happened. Writing will help me remember that my name is John—not Juan or Sassenach or scumbag or piece of shite—and that once I was treated with respect, healthy with full stomach, promising future, and a girl. No, I will not write about her today. Today I am in pain and feverish—a mistake to add regret to misery. But now I write her name everyday because I'm terrified of forgetting again. Her name is Pauli, and she is waiting for me still.

At least I know the date, thanks to the Scottish hostages who started a calendar on the wall in their quarters, a slightly improved version of my solo apartment in the hold. On occasion, they tolerate my presence. Usually, they ignore me. Donald seems to come and go at will. I believe it is he who is responsible for the meager subsistence that keeps us alive. Some of the Spanish soldiers have returned. They and the guards are to be avoided at all cost.

I've learned that the San Juan de Sicilia has been here since 25 September. Thus, the men have been stranded for a little over a month. Here we sit—what's left of a crew of three hundred—not because of weather, but to repair damage and to take on fresh supplies. The hope remains strong that this once mighty galleon will see Spain again. The Spaniards, as well as all of us on board, are at the mercy of Lachlan Maclean of Duart, who has never been known for his compassion. But he has agreed to a deal with the present captain. I don't know the details.

Back to this journal I found wrapped in cloth in a dark corner of the hold. No doubt Juan, the sailor who owned it, is blissfully dead and to be envied. Certainly, that will be all of our fate, coming sooner than later. Finding the journal and enough small bits of lead to create my own pencils may prove my salvation. In order to keep my mind active, I am working diligently to translate Juan's words—from Spanish, of course, but not the Spanish I learned long ago while studying in Spain. Fortunately for me, his handwriting is clear with beautifully formed letters—certainly far better than my spider-like scrawl.

Why am I bothering to translate? I don't always know. It gives my mind a purpose, a reason to go on. If ever I leave this miserable place and am somehow transformed to my former self, I shall publish a book telling of Juan and John's adventures. Juan's story may be the easier one to relate. How amusing that our ship is the San Juan de Sicilia! Too many Johns! One John down—two more to go; just the ship and me.

My parents are proud that I'm supporting our King Philip by joining the fight for Spain. We hate the Protestant queen, our mortal enemy. England attacks our ships and steals our treasure. We will punish it severely.

Sorry it didn't work out that way, Juan. You and your fellow countrymen were the punished ones, and it appears that I will join you. For now, my meager rationings for the day have arrived, delivered by a wasted-away deckhand who should be commended for not devouring it himself. It is barely enough to keep me alive. Today's menu of stale bread, dirty water, and a few chickpeas I'm ashamed to say I will consume with relish, before prowling around to see what I might steal. Most likely I would have starved or died of thirst if I hadn't become brave in making my way around the ship.

I have been assigned to a war galleon, one of twenty. I believe the name of our ship is a good omen for both Spain and me—the San Juan de Sicilia, the most powerful and important in the fleet. I'm proud to be on such a large, heavy vessel with three decks and three masts. I am one of 400 men. There are about 40 guns aboard, and I will be in charge of a cannon. Venganza for Spain! Venganza for Mary, Queen of Scots!

If you could see your gallant ship now, Juan! Over half of the crew is missing or dead, blood stains the decks, most of the sails barely serviceable. The Armada is crippled, scattered, hopeless. Some ships may return safely to Spain, but it is doubtful if any of the men aboard will be well again, physically or mentally.

Unlike many, I have total confidence in Captain Medina Sidonia and am proud to serve under him. All of us received written orders, which I am enclosing in this journal and will follow faithfully.

You might not have been wise to put your trust in Medina, friend Juan. He will fail you. Those orders you cherished were unbelievably difficult to translate, but I believe, in the main, I achieved it without too many errors.

First and foremost, you must all know, from the highest to the lowest, that the principal reason which has moved His Majesty to undertake this enterprise is his desire to serve God, and to convert to his church many peoples and souls who are now oppressed by the heretical enemies of our Catholic faith. I have assured King Philip that our cause is a holy one, and that Almighty God is on our side and will lead us to success.

Nothing stirs up people more than claiming God is with them. Of course, we English did the same thing. Better, I think, to be like the ancient Greeks and have many gods. Then let the gods fight their own wars and leave the people alone. An interesting thought. If that were possible, history might look quite different.

I also enjoin you to take particular care that no soldier, sailor, or other person in the Armada shall blaspheme or deny Our Lord, Our Lady, or the Saints, under severe punishment inflicted at our discretion. With regard to other less serious oaths, offenders will be punished by docking their wine ration.

Good heavens, Medina! Is that why our wine is almost gone? Has someone been saying naughtys?

As these disorders usually arise from gambling, you will endeavor to repress this as much as possible, especially the prohibited games, and allow no play at night on any account.

As if anyone has anything to gamble, dear Captain. But I am growing weary of you and my efforts. I shall try to translate more of your pompous orders at another time.

On his guard, John wandered around the ship before facing another night of restless sleep. His captors and fellow prisoners usually ignored him, but caution was always essential. He imagined some would happily kill him if it meant a scrap more bread and a sip of wine. Occasionally, captors shouted for him to do their bidding, but none seemed to have enough energy left for cruelty. Whether friend or foe, they would die together soon. He wondered when Donald would return. Donald worried him. Certainly he held the key for John's presence and how this madness would end.

Thank goodness for the journal. He would like to write all day, but what if he ran out of paper or could no longer make crude pencils? Writing must be limited to what was important. The thought of someone reading his words forced him to consider the content carefully. Too absurd to report such things as, "I'm leaving now to further pollute the waters or to forage for a scrap of moldy bread." The journal was sacred and should contain mainly the translations of Juan's records and John's memories of Pauline. Pauli. Yes, he finally remembered her name. Practically everything had come back to him. Why hadn't she been the first memory to return? Too painful, perhaps. But he must keep her alive in his heart and mind. He would not take the chance of forgetting again.

John looked out at the dark waters, lit only by a full moon. All Hallow's Eve and not even a bonfire on shore. Curious. One would expect the Celts to be out frolicking by now. Hadn't they invented Samhain? Ah, well, in a few days they would be treated to a stellar fireworks display. He shook his head, puzzled. In his own time, he had seen the site where the ship exploded and had assumed that's where it had been anchored. He should be looking out on Tobermory Bay, even though the town didn't exist in 1588. He should not see Duart Castle on the Sound of Mull. If history were to be obeyed, the San Juan de Sicilia had anchored in the wrong place. He shrugged. Nothing for him to do but return to his hole. A few sips of wine and then to sleep, perchance to dream of Pauli.

He awoke with a start, terrified at first. Shaken, covered in sweat. The dream, not about Pauli, had come unexpectedly. Instead, he relived an incident he had hoped to forget. He was nineteen again, serving in the British Navy, when the life and death goal for that day, as it had been for many, was to find the German battleship Bismarck. Once again in the dream, John was blown without mercy by a great gale. He and his fellow sailors, unsure of their bearings, hunched against the blast, certain the end had come. The captain, increasingly alarmed, cut the motor.

Suddenly, they heard voices speaking Spanish. Spain was neutral then, but they thought people might be in need of help. The voices grew unnaturally loud as they came nearer and nearer, until on the horizon a galleon appeared, like illustrations of those in the Spanish Armada. It could have been the San Juan de Sicilia, looking brand new, as if it were just beginning it's disastrous 1588 journey. The vessel came closer and closer before vanishing from sight—like a mirage.

If it had been only John who had seen and heard, he would have thought he was completely daft and kept still. But all the men had stared at each other in horror. The captain ordered total secrecy. Perhaps as an omen, the very next day John's ship sank the Bismarck.

Taking a sip of precious water, John dragged himself away from sleep and the dream. He had never told a soul what happened and had never tried to decipher the meaning of the vision. A seed had been planted, though. The Spanish Armada became part of his life, in ways both possible and impossible. He almost wished he could return to the dream. Yes, it was frightening, but at least his mates were there, all in the same boat. He smiled at his foolish idiom, but the smile didn't reach his heart. He was empty, alone, lonely. And he couldn't even remember Pauli's voice.

"Sleeping again, ye lazy lump?" Friend-enemy or enemy-friend Donald kicked him awake. "It's mid-morning, ye stowaway."

"Ouch, Donald, stop it! And a kidnapped victim isn't exactly a stowaway. What do you expect me to be doing?"

Donald actually grinned. "Fer starters, git up and meet someone."

Slowly, resentfully, he obeyed, leaving a fine dream behind.

Donald gestured toward a trembling man. "This is my oldest brother, Kenneth Ruari Maclean. Our uncle, the laird, is having his bit of fun by making Kenneth join the hostages."

"He doesnae like me," Kenneth admitted, attempting a smile.

John didn't know what to say, so he kept still.

"And this lowly ruffian claims to be English, but I'm gey sure he's a Scot."

"John Rand Burgess," he said, "but my grandmother was a Maclean."

"So ye see, Kenneth, practically next of kin."

"Aye," Kenneth said. "And just like all my kinfolk, he would cut my throat for a flask of whisky."

Donald shook his head. "This one has no cause. You may be of help to each other before too many days have passed."

John nodded, smiling in a friendly fashion. He could not afford to make enemies. He didn't tell Donald they were running out of days, that it would be over soon.

The Sea Journal
1 November 1588

All Saints Day, according to the primitive calendar on the wall. For me, it will always be the first of April, the Day of the Gowk, and the Gowk is me— the most absurd cuckoo to ever flap its wings or make a sound. The first of April 1950, and it's been so for years and years.

Today, our Spanish soldier watchdogs are off on an expedition for the Laird of Duart, Lachlan Mor Maclean, who is just using them to fight his bloody battles with the MacDonalds. The exchange of hostages continues to be most curious. On board, my fellow captives are all Macleans. I hear them arguing, often loudly, when I make my daily journey searching for food. (I spotted a few rats and am hungry enough to consider catching them.) For some reason, the hostages' wrath is directed toward Kenneth, who does not seem able to defend himself. Oddly, they believe their laird would be pleased if they turned against Kenneth, his own nephew. Donald thinks I can help his brother. How am I to do that when I can't help myself? More foolish than the Scots, though, are the Spaniards, going along with the laird's demands, even allowing some of their men to be held at the castle. But I suppose it's that or face certain death, although they must know it's likely to happen anyway.

I refuse to think about that now. Instead, I shall work on my translations. It's proving most interesting. The last entry in Juan's journal was on 7 August 1588, either three months ago or 362 years—take your pick.

Juan had been confident of success that day, certain the fierce storms beginning at five in the morning would only weaken the English. He must have been killed on 8 August at the Battle of Gravelines, a few miles from Calais.

In my research, I learned a fair amount about the battle even before I went to Tobermory. Considering my present situation, it's not surprising I'm not clear on the details. I would give a great deal to have my notes.

Although the Armada had suffered terrible losses, still optimistic Captain Sidonia expected the Duke of Parma, governor of the Spanish Netherlands, to have a large army waiting in Dunkirk, insuring them of final victory. But Parma and his army were not there. The Armada had been betrayed. What followed proved devastating.

Back then, few European country supported England. I kept bumping into parallels between that attempt to conquer England and my own war. Even some of the significant battle sites were the same. And while in theory many nations supported our war against Hitler, England often seemed very much alone. Somehow, I felt vindicated that the English had experienced at least one victory at Dunkirk.

The Armada was well and truly defeated by the English. While some accused Medina Sidonia of cowardice for not continuing the fight, he turned a deaf ear to their taunts. Too many ships were destroyed. It did not make sense to waste any more Spanish lives. Thus, Sidonia ordered the remaining ships to flee to the North Sea, beginning a hopeless retreat the long way around, seemingly their only chance. God must still be on their side, Sidonia thought. After all, He had changed the wind direction to favor them. Perhaps they could at least be led safely home with their lives, if not their pride, intact. Briefly, the English were in hot pursuit, but they were short on ammunition and certain the violent winds and storms of the North Sea would provide a definitive defeat, so they turned back.

Even before his death, my writing fellow, Juan, described some of the Spaniards' hardships.

We envy the sailors and are at their mercy. As soldiers, we thought ourselves superior to sailors, even those of us with lowly ranks. But they are accustomed to bad weather and enjoy making fun of us for not being able to manage it. I have been terribly seasick, and the odors of vomit and other filth only serve to continue my malady.

What might Juan have made of our conditions today? Perhaps he would have found his lot not quite so dreadful. I'm grateful to you, Juan. Without your accounts to decipher and this journal in which to add my own daily observations, I might have gone insane.

I must return to my cannon. The thrill of firing it has worn off, and I no longer find pleasure in screaming insults at the English. I will wet a piece of sailcloth to keep next to me to help put out the fire if a cannonball explodes nearby. It is unfortunate that I never learned to swim. I'm uncertain I could survive in these frigid waters.

Frigid waters? Mull waters in November are far worse than those of the English Channel in August. Frigid? Juan, you didn't know the meaning of the word.

Our struggle will be ended soon when our Monarch, His Majesty King Philip II ascends the throne, wears the crown, and becomes the mightiest ruler of both Spain and England. Greater even than Caesar, or Charlemagne, or Alexander the Great! It will be a glorious day, and I feel certain God will suitably reward all who have labored these many months.

War! So often a mistake. I've been thinking about wars in general. My war, which I still consider just, ended only five years ago, and now I'm caught up in this one. It's apparent to me that what drove Spain to conquer Britain was similar to what my world experienced in its fight against fascism. Both times, most European countries took sides, each one certain their lives depended on the outcome, declaring their enemies barbarous monsters and enemies of God and man. This war, so long ago, with countries siding with England or Spain, was not that different. Perhaps all wars were similar. I'm being somewhat nationalistic, but I find it interesting that the world must learn over and over that it is not wise to underestimate England. Do you suppose I should keep faith and not underestimate her, either? Would it do any good to consider a positive outcome for me?

Ah, well, it is growing too dark to see the page. Our captors have returned, out of sorts, worried about themselves and not thinking about us. Something may be about to happen, and I will welcome the change, whatever it might be. Goodnight, Pauli, sweet innocent girl with the fly-away hair, questioning eyes, and knowing smile. It is doubtful that you're anything now but a memory—may that memory linger even after death.

He was shaken roughly. "Help me! Donald said ye can be trusted."

Honestly, he was becoming tired of these rude awakenings. "Yes, Kenneth, you may trust me, but to do what? I have no authority here."

Kenneth could hardly get the words out. "I heard them. They will kill me before dawn."

"But they are Macleans, your own kin."

"Doesnae matter. They call me saftie, a jessie." His lower lip quivered.

The men might be right. Clearly, there was something amiss with Kenneth, but that was no call to kill him. He was Donald's brother, and Donald wanted him protected. But how could John help? At this point, he probably knew the ship better than anyone on board, except the Spaniards. Most likely, both sides were in a drunken state, thanks to the laird's generous supply of whisky, and not to be feared at the moment.

"Follow me, Kenneth, and don't make any noise." John had a glimmer of an idea. Yes, no one was near the remaining lifeboat. Security on board had become nonexistent. With Kenneth finally exerting a small amount of courage and much strength, they lowered the boat to the water, and Kenneth climbed down.

"I thank ye, my friend," Kenneth said. "Will ye nae come with me?"

John considered. No doubt he would still face danger on land, but at least he wouldn't be blown up in three days. Voices. Someone coming. "Go," he hissed. "Now."

"But . . ."

"Too late. Go now. Quietly." John hid behind a large barrel and waited.

"Ah, yer a numpty. No one is here. Takin' us from our rest. I should clobber you."

John waited until all was still again before returning to the hold.

The Sea Journal
2 November 1588

I will be matter of fact and impersonal today. I must not allow myself to dwell on Kenneth—that the lifeboat and my last chance of escape are gone. Depression comes too easily, and despair does not suit my temperament. I shall stick to my translations of Juan's extravagant expectations.

Spain is the mightiest ruler of the seas. Nothing will stop us from victory.

Early days then, Juan. You should see your powerful galleon now. Wrecked. Hopelessly beyond repair, sails torn, lifeboats and oars gone. Most of your comrades died violently. It's a pity that I know exactly what will happen soon. Your ship will explode, Juan—whether by accident or deliberate plot might never be determined—and pieces of it will remain at the bottom of these waters for centuries, causing people to wonder what treasures may be hidden. Aren't you lucky you were spared this? But I imagine the way you met your end was not especially pleasant.

It is no use. I'm succeeding only in both frightening and boring myself, if such a combination is possible. Who am I kidding? The situation is hopeless. I'm writing for myself alone. No one will ever read this journal, unless another poor soul also trapped in time comes along. (Hello, poor soul, whoever you might be. Do carry on. I shall try to leave some pages and a few additional primitive pencils, if I can locate more pieces of lead.) Now I will write about the only person who still matters.

Pauline . . . Pauli . . . For as many days or minutes I have left, I shall think of her, I shall love her. Instead of the memories being painful, perhaps they'll give me some comfort tonight. It might be clichéd, a Romeo and Juliet notion, to say I loved her at first glance, but I believe that is close to what happened. At least I loved her by third glance. She seemed so fragile and alone at the bus depot, perusing the brochures, wondering if there was anything she might do in spite of the dreary day. At first I thought she was much younger—perhaps seventeen or eighteen. Then she looked up at me, and I saw the possibility of a brave, determined woman behind those brilliant blue eyes. Her lustrous hair pleased me most when it was wild and windblown. In fact, I loved her best when she was wild and windblown.

The only time I ever saw her proper, formal, and tame was at that horrible dinner party her parents attended, when her hair was swept up high into a determined fashionable style. All of her that night seemed brittle and phony. Could that be when I fell in love with her—when I realized her discomfort was from excruciating embarrassment. Out of her fear that I would think less of her because of her parents' behavior, she retreated deep inside herself. I became eager to care for her. I longed to be the knight in shining armor she seemed to see in me.

Those parents, Angelica and Harvey, were perfectly disgraceful, and she would have been completely at their mercy when I disappeared. How did they protect you? What a foolish question. They didn't. And what did you think when I vanished? Did you believe I had left you willingly? You had so little self-confidence, you might very well have thought just that. Enough! I must not dwell on what will tear me apart. Please, Pauli, know in your heart that nothing could be further from the truth.

Pauli, I should have told you about my family. You might have been less anguished about your own. My father, an army deserter, spent the war in prison until he had the good sense to die of typhus. My mother, pathetic soul, never had an opinion to call her own, until she developed a questionable backbone and took a great overdose of sleeping pills. After her death, my young brother and sisters became wastrels, whom I have no interest in seeing ever again. The times I attempted to help my mother and siblings, I was considered an interfering know-it-all. I tried—it's over. You, Pauli, are the only family I want.

Did I know Pauli was the girl of my heart and dreams at the Chocolate Shop when she ate all those biscuits with complete abandon, without any pretense of watching her weight or some other female notion? Usually, her smile was slight and knowing, a Mona Lisa almost-smile. Occasionally, though, she would forget herself, and her whole face became as bright as sunshine, her laughter exhuberant. Oddly, she truly believed she wasn't smart, but I knew differently. Pauli thirsted for knowledge, reading everything she could. I could tell she had started to study the Armada just so she could converse with me. It was certain I would marry her when she joined the seals in clapping, she with her hands, they with their flippers. Her joy filled my heart. She was my own even before we made our magical, non-seeing trip to Staffa and before I held her in my arms during that precious night that was supposed to be one of many. Pauli thought I was intelligent and wonderful, when she was perfection itself. She may no longer exist anywhere, of course, but perhaps I don't, either. When I'm able, I look to the shore, so different from what I remember, and pretend I see her—at the hotel that isn't there, walking along a nonexistent road, sipping tea in the ancient castle. And then I grow afraid, wondering how I'll continue to exist if I no longer can even pretend to see her.

Foraging among the passed-out hostages, he located a meager breakfast. Their rage against Kenneth taking the last lifeboat had ended in drunken stupors. They were unlikely to remember what had come of the leftover bread and wine. John had returned and was about to begin his translations for the day when an unexpected visitor entered the hold—Donald, not alone. A terrified young boy was with him.

"Juan or Sean or whatever you're calling yourself, this lad needs your help. Make certain he is properly clothed and hide him the best ye can."

"Who is he, Donald? Do you know his name?"

"Aye, that I do, but ask him yourself, and then decide if you believe. I do, but many the time a'm aff ma heid."

John nodded, understanding too well about being off in the head, but he would deal with the boy later. "Did Kenneth . . . ?"

"Aye, a thousand blessings on you, Maclean. Kenneth is back and hidden safely. He is a good brother but not a' that cannie."

John suspected that Kenneth was retarded, a condition not handled well in his time, either. "I'm glad I could help," he said simply.

"Now this lad will help you. Donald patted the boy on the shoulder. "Be brave, young Maclean. Now I go before those lazy louts come to life again."

John and the boy stared at each other, trying to take each other's measure.

John helped the new hostage out of his faded dungarees and Clan Maclean jacket, certainly a dangerous thing to wear in his present situation. He carried a yellow Mackintosh similar to John's. Standing vulnerable in only his vest and briefs, he shook all over, possibly responding to cold as well as fear.

"Relax, lad," John said. "You're as safe as any of us. I'll find you something different to wear. You're rather small, but some of the dead soldiers and sailors were undersized. Their clothing was saved before they were tossed to the fish."

The boy said nothing, but his eyes said clearly that John's words were not comforting. Tread more carefully, John cautioned. He seemed to have lost the ability to be tactful. After all, being forced to wear dead men's clothes hadn't pleased him, either. "What is your name?" he asked gently.

"Lachlan Maclean, but everyone calls me Lachie." Then he fell apart. "Please take me back to Francie! She's waiting for me in the castle. By now, she must be so scared, and I'm scared, too."

Sadly, John shook his head. "I wish I could, Lachie Maclean, but I'm afraid I don't have the power. You and I have landed in a bit of a stew. You're American, aren't you, despite your Scottish name? Where are you from?" Lachie mentioned a town in New York State. "Well, Lachie, for as long as we're able, we'll stick together. I'm from England, so I'm not very popular on this ship. As an American, you aren't likely to be, either. To these people, your country doesn't exist yet."

From a small storage room in the hold, John found some loosely fitting woolen breeches—with a length of rope for a belt—and a jerkin to wear on top. Then he added a floppy hat to hide a hairstyle that would be foreign even in 1950. Lachie looked foolish but would pass muster if examined. His speech would not.

"Pretend to be a mute. Don't speak when there's anyone around but me."

Lachie nodded. "You and Donald."

"Are you hungry?"

"Yes, I didn't have lunch. Francie and I were going to have tea with an old lady as soon as I came up from the dungeons. Except I never went up again. I came here."

"Duart Castle." The dungeons of Duart! John held tightly to a beam to keep from falling. He didn't wait for confirmation—it was obvious. He and Lachie had gone through a similar experience. But before they went foraging for food, there was one more question that needed asking. "Back where you came from— what year was it? What was the date?"

"April first," Lachie said. "The first of April 2004."

So far in the future! How could that be? But the same day he had come to this unholy place—in 1950. "The first of April. The Day of the Gowk."

"Yes, I know all about that. Angus Black told us."

Angus Black? That wasn't possible. He couldn't still be alive—certainly not in 2004. A great rage swept over him. John grabbed the boy by the throat. "Stop telling lies! Right this minute! What is the date? Why are you here? Who sent you? You couldn't know Angus Black!"

As Lachie began to choke, John backed off. He'd scared the child. Truthfully, he'd scared himself. "I'm sorry," he said, voice shaking. "I knew an Angus Black many years ago. Fifty-four years, if you're telling the truth. And he was an old man then."

Lachie turned the corner from fear to anger—possibly a healthy move. "Everyone wants to talk about fifty-four years! Well, back home, it *is* 2004. And Angus Black did tell me about the April Gowk; it's like our April Fools' Day but it lasts 48 hours. I'm not lying, and I want to eat something and then go back to our hotel! I miss Francie, and I don't like you!" He began to sob, the brief sprint of anger spent.

John homed in on the newest information. "Hotel? What hotel? Tell me, if you want food." Had he meant it to sound like a threat? What was wrong with him?

"Okay," Lachie sniffled. "We're staying at the Western Isles, the best hotel in town."

John found some stale bread and gave him his own share of wine. The wine put Lachie right to sleep. That was good; he needed to think. And he wanted to write.

The Sea Journal
3 November 1588

Such an unusual event—in a place where little changes. I don't know if I should be glad or disheartened. The laird's nephew, Donald Maclean, came on board with another young boy. Although dressed similarly to me when I first arrived, he was not wearing children's clothing from 1950, either. What is certain, neither of us belong in 1588. Donald insisted that I take the lad under my wing, and I had no choice but to agree.

Since I boarded a few days or many years ago, Donald has saved my life on various occasions. The Spaniards or the Scots surely would have put me to death if it hadn't been for Donald's intervention. Neither side has much taste for Englishmen. My rescue of Kenneth seems to have evened the score with Donald. He and I are approaching friendship. But this new lad, Lachie Maclean, how can he possibly help? And what shall I make of him?

Both of us are trapped in a time warp; me from 1950 without any notion of how long I have been here—possibly for fifty-four years, as improbable as that is. I had thought 362 years separated my time from the Spanish Armada, but if Lachie is correct, it had actually been—I did some quick figuring—416 years. No matter. Both are impossible scenarios. I will question him further once he awakens. Meanwhile, I'll attempt more translations to take my spinning mind off the new complications.

When I reach home again, may Our Lady of Mercy be with me, I will explain to my young brother how to load a cannon. He will be properly impressed.

Certainly Juan was impressed with himself, and I am impressed with me. Although the translating is exhausting, it's also worthwhile and becoming easier.

I regret parting with my wine and wonder if the lack will keep me awake. Soon, I will close my eyes and find out. Pauli, if I have been here for fifty-four years, you are surely long departed. I must bring the dream of you to an end. If it weren't for Lachie to consider, I would kill myself.

Is that what Donald meant? Will Lachie be the means of saving me, now that I must take care of him? I would not have credited Donald with that much wisdom.

John shivered. The 4th of November—the next to their last day—all was eerily silent onboard, as if the ship itself knew it was doomed. John would not kid himself that what was coming would be good for anyone—Scottish hostages or Spanish sailors and soldiers. He wondered how many people were actually on the ship at the moment. He and Lachie were still alone in their quiet corner. Lachie would awaken soon, hungry, but it was doubtful anything would come their way. Tomorrow, of course, if history could be believed, it would all be over. Will I burn to death or drown, John wondered? Or perhaps he would magically transport back to 1950. That was a new thought—a hope to hang on to. Perhaps he was meant to die in his own time.

Ultimately, the ship would blow up, by accident or design. probably tomorrow, 5 November. No escape for any of them—unless the men's calendar was wrong or history was mistaken or John tried to intervene. He shook his head. Attempting to change the past? Probably not a good idea. What else might be affected?

While waiting for Lachie to awaken or for food that might or might not arrive, he returned to Juan's words. There would not be many opportunities left.

The Sea Journal
4 November 1588

I am convinced that Francis Drake is the wickedest person to ever walk the earth. The English queen has knighted him, but I would knife him. He is no Sir, no knight. He is nothing but a cutthroat pirate. If we had nothing against the English but Drake, I would fight to my last breath. El Draque's attack on our ships at Cadiz cost my older brother, Diego, his life. I will avenge Diego. It is the only thing left I can do for him.

Poor Juan, you were no match for Drake or any of them. I understand your point of view. You were correct. Drake was more of a scoundrel than a hero. He was called a privateer, which was just a fancy word for a pirate with a license. He stole Spanish possessions, although that point is debatable, considering the Spanish had stolen silver and gold from Peru. No doubt, dysentery was a deserved ending for Sir Francis Drake. I remember a poem about him I wrote when I was a young student.

> *Francis Drake, the pirate,*
> *Was a nasty fearsome rake*
> *He tried to trick the Spanish*
> *Never giving them a break.*
>
> *"Sir Francis Drake's a privateer,"*
> *Declared the mighty queen,*
> *"Pirate sounds too common,*
> *Although he's plenty mean.*
>
> *"He sails around the world, you know,*
> *To find me jewels and gold.*
> *Don't tell me how does these things,*
> *Just say he's bloody bold."*
>
> *El Draco, the Dragon,*
> *Was feared both far and near,*
> *Attacking ships his favorite sport*
> *Preferring that to beer.*
>
> *Spain's King Philip heard the threat,*
> *He'd destroy that wretched Draco,*
> *"The greatest Armada ever formed*
> *Will conquer soon this rascal.*
>
> *"England always thinks it's best,*
> *And Queenie did betray me,*

Spain is master of revenge—
Such puny ships will flee."

But those puny ships the Spaniards scorned,
Knew well the English waves.
Drake and friends would play their bowls,
Time later to be brave.

Now—"Fire ships forward, flames to their masts!"
"We're doomed!" Spain's captain glared at his map,
"Head North for home," he ordered, "and better make it fast!"
"The seas will finish off those Sods," Drake laughed. "I'll take a nap."

An awful poem! But my teacher seemed to like it, after she made me clean up the language a bit. Unfortunately, Lachie is waking. He will be hungry, poor lad, and any food coming our way is certain to be inedible. I wonder if the poem might amuse him.

The Sea Journal
5 November 1588

Before Lachie and I consider yet another day without food and before he awakens, I will tackle another translation. I feel as if I know Juan, and occasionally mourn his death—during the times I'm not contemplating my own. Today might be the blessed ending, although I will not share that information with the boy. I will also keep from him today's date. For someone his age, he seems to know a great deal of history.

Remember, remember!
The fifth of November,
The gunpowder treason and plot;
I know of no reason the gunpowder treason
Should ever be forgot!

Doubtful that Lachie knew that old verse I learned as a schoolboy. Americans don't know much about Guy Fawkes Day. Interesting that James was King of England back then, and here in 1588, a different James is King of Scotland. Oh, well . . . *Holloa, boys! Holloa! God save the King!* Lachie would know what the fifth of November meant for the Armada, though.

I must return to Juan. Soon I will run out of time to translate—or to do anything else.

We are bound for Calais, where 21,000 troops will board our ships, and then we will take them across the Channel. Invasion is certain, and I feel confident that victory is ours.

I'm not sorry you didn't succeed, Juan, but I am sorry you died. You went quickly, without pain, I hope. You have been my only friend on board—until now. In some ways it is good to be needed again, if only for the short time we have left.

"Mr. Burgess, I'm hungry."

Lachie was awake. "So am I," John said, putting the journal aside. "Possibly someone will bring us food later." To try to keep both their minds occupied and off empty stomachs, John encouraged Lachie to talk about himself. "While we're waiting, shall we get to know each other better? Tell me about your family. You haven't mentioned your mother."

"She died. I don't remember her much. That makes me sad sometimes."

"I'm sorry." Not a good subject. "Your father?" A better topic, it seemed. His father was a businessman, supporting interesting projects. In Lachie's time, 2004, he was in charge of a diving expedition to discover Spanish treasure.

"That seems kind of strange to me now," Lachie said. "Because we're here, and I don't think there's any treasure, do you?"

John shook his head. He did not. "Although there are parts of the ship I haven't seen, but I wouldn't invest any money."

Lachie nodded. "My dad did. Lots. I wish I could tell him the divers won't find anything. Maybe he could get his money back."

And Pauli's father, too, John reflected, although what he knew of the man made him feel he had it coming. "Well, as I said, there are parts of the ship we don't know anything about. I suppose there's still a chance they'll find a treasure."

John refrained from telling Lachie what would happen soon to the galleon. It would explode mysteriously, and everyone on board would be killed—by fire or water. Which ending would he prefer? Drowning, most likely. But now, because of Lachie's presence, neither one was acceptable. Was there the slightest possibility they could escape or be rescued? No chance, he decided. He had been silent too long, and Lachie was growing restless. John must keep his mind from wandering into dark places.

"You mentioned someone named Francie. Is she your sister?"

"Francie is my friend. She takes care of me when Dad has trips and meetings."

"You like her?"

Tears came. "Yeah, she's cool." From Lachie's expression, John determined that cool meant something different from *keep cool* and that it was a good thing. "Once when we were seal watching, we looked over the dock, and a seal jumped up and stared right into my face." Through the tears, he started to laugh, the first time since he'd come to this godforsaken hole. "It was so funny! Have you ever gone seal watching?"

To John's dismay, he felt his own tears forming. "Oh, yes."

"Poor Francie. She must be so scared about me. Maybe the Broken Lady will help her."

"Broken lady?"

"That's what I used to call her. Only Francie and I helped fix her a little. A lot of people call her Miss Proper, but her real last name is Porter—Miss Pauline Porter."

Pauline. Was it possible? John's heart beat louder than Juan's cannons. "Is she a small, beautiful woman with shiny golden hair?"

Lachie giggled. "No way! She's got gray hair in a bun, and she's old. She goes to Tobermory every single March—but not because she likes it there. Francie and Angus say it's a very sad story."

Of course, if she were indeed his Pauli, and Lachie knew her in 2004, she would be in her seventies. But if John could believe the reflection he saw occasionally, he'd remained a shabby version of himself, still the same age.

"Lachie, what do you remember about how you got here? It could be important. I'd like to compare your memories with mine."

"It's kind of fuzzy now." Fuzzy—a good word. "Francie hurt her ankle and couldn't go up or down the stairs of the castle. She told me I could go to the roof all by myself."

John couldn't recall the roof. He probably hadn't had time to go there. "What happened next?"

"On the roof, I met some boys who invited me to go with them to the dungeons. I asked Francie, and she said okay."

Those dungeons—dark, damp, smelling of evil. What John couldn't remember at that moment was why he was there. Didn't he know before? Fuzzy, Lachie's word, certainly applied to him. He knew he was supposed to meet Pauli but for some reason didn't. And then all went blank until he woke up on this ship with a bandaged head. "And then?"

"I was in the dungeon, but the boys were gone. I saw some Spanish hostage figures. I thought they were made of wax, but they came to life and grabbed me. I was scared and wanted to go back to Francie. Then a boy who looked like me came running down the stairs. He brought me here."

"Donald," John said.

"Donald," Lachie agreed. Then he clutched his stomach. "I'm really hungry, Mr. Burgess."

"There may not be anything on board, but go ahead and see if you can find food. Be careful, though. Take no chances. If you hear anyone, hide."

It is doubtful that Lachie heard anything but the word, "food," for he scrambled away quickly. John was debating whether to take a nap or return to the journal when he heard angry voices.

"Get yer filthy hands off me!"

Had Lachie been discovered? No, the voice belonged to Donald Maclean, who was being handled roughly by a black-bearded Spaniard. Stay away, Lachie, John prayed.

Donald was thrust into the hold, and the Spaniard left. Cautioning him to remain silent, John held up his finger. "Lachie," he mouthed silently. For what seemed like hours, they waited until Lachie finally returned.

"Oh, good, Donald's here. I couldn't find any food. Did you bring some?"

"Never mind food. It isnae important now. Or at least it isnae as important as your lives. Listen carefully if ye value them."

To John's horror, Donald confirmed that he had been captured. The Spanish captain had refused to keep his agreement with the laird. After attacking the MacDonalds, the Spaniards came back on board with Maclean's blessings. But that wasn't the entire agreement. The laird had provided whisky, wine, and what meager food had been consumed, but the Spaniards had promised to pay for it in gold. Then the captain changed his mind. He would not pay. Furious, Maclean's men took three officers back to the castle as hostages.

"The laird, my uncle, has sent me to collect the gold, but the foul blackguards captured me." He was about to say more when all three lurched forward.

"We're moving!" Lachie cried.

"The captain is sailing without keeping his bargain. I will not allow that to happen, even if it means death. I will defend the honor of Clan Maclean!"

Lachie's mouth dropped. "What are you going to do?"

Something involving a large explosion, John imagined, and it made sense that they were moving. The San Juan de Sicilia was sailing closer to its final resting place off Tobermory Bay. But would Donald give them a choice of fire or water? Would John and Lachie burn to death or drown?

Donald started to leave, then turned back. "Out of time, ye came here," he said. "I don't know how or why, but the blame for you, young Lachlan, is mine. You, John, saved Kenneth's life, and I am in your debt. Ye are both Macleans, my kin. You must follow my orders. I cannae promise you'll make it back to your own time, but I will try." Donald stood quietly, thinking. "Sneak to the aft part of the ship and find my wee boat. Hide under the tarp. Wait 'til nightfall. As soon as you hear a loud whistle, row away from here, toward Duart Castle. Mind that side door where we came out, Lachie?"

"I think so."

"Ye must. It is the way back. Ken ye well to row the second ye hear me whistle. There'll no be time after. And Lachie, my brother, stay faithful and true tae the Clan Maclean!"

Lachie nodded.

"And what about you, Donald Maclean?" John asked.

"Dinnae fash yersel' wit me, my friend," was all Donald said.

"Try to return with us."

"Aye." And then he was gone.

John grabbed the sea journal, put his arm around a bewildered Lachie, and led him to the lifeboat. "Keep hope, lad," he said, "and you might consider praying."

Hidden under the tarp, John wrote these last words.

The Sea Journal
5 November 1588

This may be the last entry of the Sea Journal, started by Juan and, if unimaginable luck is with him, completed someday by John Rand Burgess. The date is 5 November 1588, and I imagine we are about to experience a different gunpowder plot. Instead of Guy Fawkes attempting to blow up Parliament in 1605, we'll have young Donald Maclean, lighting a powder keg, ending his life, as well as the Spanish soldiers and sailors. And, of course, sinking their gold bullion, if it existed. A fiery revenge indeed for Clan Maclean!

A shrill whistle in the distance. An uncertain pause. Then a boy's frantic scream. "Go!"

Lachie and John

November 5, 1588 & April 4, 2004

DEAFENING EXPLOSIONS LIT THE NIGHT sky, yet they still managed to keep the small craft upright on the turbulent sea. Finally fires ended. The first thing John and Lachie noticed was bitter cold from the wind and waves. No longer mild, early November. Then they noticed other boats—on the water and in the distance along the shore. And lights, not from fires or the moon, but from light bulbs! Lights scattered everywhere! Instead of being pitch black, the entire island seemed dotted with lights. They could see the castle clearly now. All signs of Donald's revenge had vanished.

"Donald, we didn't save him!" Lachie was sobbing, heartbroken.

"We couldn't, Lachie. If we had waited longer, we would have died, too."

"He was our friend. He saved us."

"Yes, he did, and we'll always be grateful. But today is the fifth of November in 1588. Do you know what that means?"

Lachie gasped. "The day the ship exploded! Why didn't we stop it?"

"Think, Lachie. Why didn't we?"

He shook his head.

"The laird was furious his orders hadn't been obeyed. He would have killed everyone, claiming any valuables on board for himself."

"Donald might have stayed alive."

"But we wouldn't. And do you think the Spaniards would have allowed Donald to live?"

"No . . ."

"He knew what was at stake and died quickly. We are a long way from safe ourselves. We need to carry on."

Reaching the shore, they abandoned their craft, now a foreign object, without bothering to anchor it down. For certain, the one thing they did not want to do was return to the burning remains of the San Juan de Sicilia.

The castle was farther away than it appeared, even though they had been rowing in its direction. Surely it would be closed, and no buses would be operating this late—even if they had money. John checked his clothing. He still wore his rags, and his pockets were empty of everything except the sea journal. Amazingly, he still had that.

"I believe we're somewhere between Tobermory and Duart Castle," John said. "Shall we go to the Western Isles instead?"

Lachie shook his head. "No, we should do what Donald said. We must find the door on the side of the castle—the one he opened when he took me to the galleon." When John looked skeptical, Lachie added, "I don't think we're all the way back. We don't belong yet."

John went along with him, although he thought it was a long shot that a small side door from 1588 would still be there in . . . whatever year this was. At least Lachie was thinking clearly again. "Lead on," he said.

Without food or clean water for so long, the man and boy dragged themselves over the last steep hill to the castle. The lights were on for security purposes only; surely there was no one around. Finally, although it was covered with dead vines and weeds, Lachie found the hidden door with its rusty handle. He and John struggled and pulled until, with great creaks and groans, the ancient door opened, and they were back in the dungeon.

The mock hostages in the cell clearly were made of wax, and they made no startling moves in their direction, although Lachie reached through the bars and touched one, just to make sure. Looking back, he could no longer see the door. Then he and John, still weak and shaky, climbed the turnpike stairs and entered the Grand Hall—into daylight—where they became two of many tourists examining the armor and swords. Lachie couldn't help hoping that time had stood still and that Francie would be sitting there waiting for him. That didn't seem likely, though, with John still with him and considering what they were wearing . . . But John's clothes! Then Lachie looked down.

"Our clothes!" he cried.

Yes, once more he was wearing his jeans and Maclean tartan jacket and carrying his weatherproof raincoat. And John in his suit looked exactly as he had in 1950 when he had finished his interviews and was on his way to have tea with Pauli. Again, he carried his mac and the briefcase containing his interview notes.

John felt his clothing, hoping, but the sea journal was gone. He guessed it was too much to expect—transporting an object from one time to another. But he took a quick look in his briefcase, and there it was. Still with him—for now. And his wallet was safe inside his suitcoat pocket. "What do you say we take the next bus to Tobermory?" he asked.

"Can we get some food first? I'm starving!"

"Good idea." John pulled a few loose coins from his pocket. Perhaps they could purchase some buns and two cups of tea before carrying on.

Lachie examined the coins. "That's your money?"

"Don't worry," John said, opening his wallet. "I have some pound notes. But we shouldn't need more than a few shillings."

Lachie examined one of the bills. "That's not what money looks like—not anymore. This doesn't even have a picture of Queen Elizabeth on it; I don't know who that dude is." Lachie thought he'd seen similar old money in the rock and coin shop in town—shillings, half-crowns, pence, things like that. "I don't think your money will work, and I don't have any."

That dude was King George. Damn! What year was this? John looked around. The Grand Hall was not quite as he remembered, and the women tourists should be wearing dresses, coats, and hats—not slacks. The men weren't in suits but denim trousers and undershirts with cartoons and odd sayings on them. Obviously, this was not 1950. Not only was his money outdated, so was he. "I feel rather like one of your fellow New Yorkers—Rip Van Winkle. Never mind, we'll get something to eat at the hotel. Do you think the bus driver will take my money?"

Lachie shrugged. "I don't think so. Only collectors want that stuff."

"Then we start walking." And hope someone will give us a lift, John thought. The distance between Duart Castle and Tobermory was twenty-four miles. Could either of them in their condition handle such a trek? At least it wasn't raining. Not that he had a vote, but he would have preferred returning to 1950. That would have been better for everyone. Lachie would simply disappear and not be born for years and years. And John would carry on where he'd left off with Pauli, sparing her years of grief. He supposed the gods knew what they were doing, but why did he still look as he had fifty-four years ago? He was the same—well, maybe more stooped over than usual—just malnourishment and fatigue . . . nothing to worry about.

Lachie hadn't paid much attention to the bus ride from Tobermory before, but he and Francie had stopped at Torosay Castle first. It seemed to him, though, that it would take a long, long time to walk all the way to the hotel. One mile later, he was sure of it. He thought about complaining, but after glancing at John, decided to keep his mouth shut. John was having an even harder time—walking slowly, taking frequent breaks—and he was starting to look different. It made sense that his beard and long hair had disappeared, but not that there was only a little bit left on his head, and it was white.

Panting, John stopped again. "Just a few minutes while I catch my breath." He sat on a stump by the side of the road. What was wrong with him? Yes, he was out of condition, but he'd walked this distance hundreds of times. What would they do if he couldn't go on? A premonition, perhaps, but he wondered if he might not be able to keep the sea journal safe. "Lachie, you carry my briefcase. If anything happens, please give it to your friend Francie."

Puzzled, Lachie took the case. "Well, okay, but . . ."

Then, the minor miracle. A farmer about to pass stopped and opened the door of his truck. "Might ye be wanting a lift?" he called out.

"Yes!" Lachie took charge, helping John to his feet and into the truck.

John wheezed slightly, then rested back next to the driver. "We're very grateful to you," he said.

"You do seem tuckered out. Did you nae wish to take the bus?"

"I lost my wallet," John lied, knowing the truth was not possible.

"Too bad, mate. Where might ye be headed? I'm going to Tobermory."

"Perfect," John said. "That's our destination, too." But as to what they would find there or what would happen next, he couldn't begin to imagine. He closed his eyes, knowing he had to rest, hoping he wouldn't fall asleep. Lachie, he thought. Lachie must be the only consideration. Lachie was only eight while he was . . . how old? He did the math. It wasn't possible. But he looked at gnarled hands he no longer recognized, gasped at the reflection in the side view mirror, and faced the truth. He was eighty-one, malnourished for many days or years, and had escaped a burning ship. And after taking a long, difficult walk, he had attempted another twenty-four miles. He wondered if he would live long enough to see Pauli again.

Lachie frowned. He should be happy because the scary time was over, but what was happening to his friend? John looked like a different person, old. His money was wrong and so were his clothes. Even though they were not in style, they'd looked okay back at the castle, but now they were way too big. They just hung on him. Lachie shrugged. He knew that some crazy thing had caused them to go from 2004 to 1588 and back again. He tried to figure it out, but the best he could do was maybe the times were different for John. Well, it would be okay. They would be with Francie soon, and she would make it right again. She would sort it all out.

Francie

T HE BORROWED DAYS WERE OVER. As far as I was concerned back then, almost everything was over for Pauline and me, and most likely for Lachie, too. But I refused to give in. Instead, I would hold on to hope, although not in the yearning way Pauline had grasped at it for fifty-four years. That would lead to despair. I must not allow reality to escape me but continue to pray, remaining optimistic that Lachie was still alive. However, I would not imagine him a part of my life ever again, and I would never return to Tobermory.

Pauline probably wouldn't come back, either, at least not during the borrowed days. "I'm a pathetic old fool. Because of four days in 1950, I've wasted my life chasing a romantic impossibility. John probably left on purpose. He was marking time until he had his way with me, and then he no longer required more. He never really loved me; he's probably married and has six grandchildren. I'll never know what my life could have been if I hadn't allowed the years to slip by."

I didn't say anything. Although I doubted that had been John's fate, I agreed with her conclusion. She might have led a happy, productive life—if her parents had been more understanding, supportive and, well, decent like my parents. If only they had cared about Pauline instead of their own imagined importance, or if only her baby girl had lived, Pauline could have been the one married with six grandchildren. If only . . . Too many if onlys! I wondered briefly what had happened to Harvey and Angelica Porter. I wouldn't ask Pauline. Certainly, they were long dead and best forgotten. As for John, Pauline could be right. He might have been a rake. In that case, what if she were to find him again? Then she would no longer have even the dream of him. If nothing else, at least she had long ago memories to cherish.

"What's next for you?" was all I dared ask.

"I'll continue to live in my house in London. It's comfortable, and a few of the neighbors are friendly. I might purchase a summer home in Tobermory. I've come here so many times I might miss it if it were gone completely. It will take time to determine how I feel. But as terrible as this experience was, Francie, you must put it behind you. Many endure tragedies far greater and manage to carry on."

I knew that. But, like Pauline, I, too, needed time to adjust. My bags were packed. No sign of me remained anywhere at the Western Isles. Rory wanted me gone as soon as possible. He had returned to Edinburgh, attending more meetings about the planned dives, although he checked in often with police. He had called me irresponsible and several ugly names I'd never repeat. It was hard to remember ever liking him, much less envisioning a romantic future. Actually, I thought he was the irresponsible one—dumping an eight-year-old kid into a foreign boarding school, and then giving someone so young and inexperienced (me) the total care of him. A dreadful father, and I wished I had the nerve to tell him what I thought—not that it would accomplish anything.

"Our taxi will arrive soon," I said to Pauline. "The day is pleasant, for a change. I'll wait outside." Our bags were downstairs already.

"Don't put too much strain on that ankle," Pauline warned. I had graduated to a walking boot and was making progress. Pauline wanted to find Angus for one last farewell. Both of us would miss him.

This was truly the end of an era for Pauline, although I was relieved she'd finally decided the waiting was over. I might have been partially responsible for her change of heart. She visualized me, coming year after year during the borrowed days, on the off chance Lachie would return. She thought of me blindly hoping, following in her steps, until I ended up as she had—forever alone.

I hobbled to the back of the hotel, where a path slopes down into town. It was almost spring at last and such a relief to no longer need a raincoat. If you had gone simply by that day's weather, you would have sworn the last six days had never happened. How I wished that were so.

The view of the bay was breathtaking, a complete glittering panorama. I could see a few boats way out. Also visible was the exact spot where the Tobermory Galleon, the San Juan de Sicilia, had exploded over 400 years ago. The divers would begin their exploration in just a few days, even though most people doubted that anything of value would be recovered. I shrugged. Maybe it was pursuing the dream that counted, although it seemed a foolhardy, expensive dream. Perhaps . . .

I stopped woolgathering. Dropping my purse, I began to tremble. In the distance, I clearly saw a boy running up the path—straight toward me. It couldn't be, but it was. It was . . . It was . . . "Pauline!" I screamed louder than I'd ever screamed before. Like a deranged banshee! "Pauline, come here! Now!"

She heard me. Doubtless, all of Tobermory heard me. And then the boy threw down a briefcase he was carrying and flung himself into my arms, nearly knocking me to the ground.

"Francie, I'm back! Did you miss me? I had an adventure. Most of it was awful, but some of it was fun and exciting."

Pauline and I couldn't hug him hard enough. He was filthy from head to toe, but it didn't matter. "What happened? Where were you?" I cried.

"I'll tell you everything," Lachie said. "But first can I have something to eat? I'm starving. And I really have to go to the bathroom!"

We started to lead him into the hotel, but he stopped suddenly. "Oh, I almost forgot. We have to wait for my friend."

"Your friend?"

"Yes, he helped me come back. He was with me, but then he said I should go ahead. He was so slow. He couldn't keep up anymore. Francie, it was scary. He looks different now. He got old—all of a sudden."

I had a crazy thought, a hunch, probably complete nonsense. But just in case, Lachie should not be a witness. "Go inside before you wet your pants," I told him. "Angus will be happy you've returned and give you something to eat." He dashed inside. Pauline and I stood waiting, quiet, wondering if we could possibly expect a miracle.

Then—"I see him," Pauline said quietly. Then she shrieked, "I see him! Johnny!"

At seventy-five, Pauline didn't exercise, much less run. But she ran then. Down the path she raced, faster than I could go, with her hair falling out of its bun, changing color, flowing like wild honey behind her.

You won't believe what happened next. I don't always believe it myself, but how could my eyes betray me so?

Pauli and her Johnny, two very old people, embraced, and as I stood on the hill with tears streaming down my face, I saw them change. I saw them become young and beautiful, until they returned to the way they must have been when they parted fifty-four years before. First, John fastened a sprig of white heather into Pauline's golden hair, and then, with their arms around each other, they drifted away, faded out of sight—forever.

Francie

2018

THE YEARS PASSED. I MARRIED Gary Stevens, the man I thought a likely consolation prize back in naive times. He became my blue ribbon, my first prize everything. I've told him what happened in Tobermory and, bless his heart, Gary loves me enough to believe it. He's also had the benefit of reading one of my dearest possessions, a sea journal. Gary encouraged me to write and publish the story. "Everyone will think it's fiction," he said. "Doesn't matter. You'll know the truth." He added that *The Borrowed Days* was the only sensible title.

Writing became a catharsis for me, as the experience had never been far from my mind—especially the ending. After seeing the reunited couple drift magically into nothing, I told Angus and Lachie, for they were the only ones likely to believe. I did not envy Lachie trying to explain things to his father and the police, but I didn't stay to find out how that went. It was time to go home.

That December, I received a Christmas card from Lachie, addressed by an unknown hand, in which he said that he had been forbidden to contact me further. I was sad about that, for I was fond of him. I spent years hoping his life turned out well. Then, recently, an unexpected phone call came from Lachlan Maclean, age twenty-two, older than I when I first went to Scotland. He had read an article about the upcoming book and had managed to track me down. His father, Rory, had married the wretched fiancée, but the marriage hadn't lasted. After years spent in various boarding schools, Lachie was finishing his degree in Oceanography at the University of North Carolina. We didn't have much to say to each other, although I was thrilled to receive the call. "I'll never forget what happened back then, Francie." I assured him I wouldn't either, and that was the end of the conversation. I doubted I would hear from him again.

No, I would never forget, and it took me years to forgive myself: an inexperienced young adult without the strength to disappoint a child, with repercussions that could have been tragic. The only positive result for me was the ability to say no firmly to my own children.

Because of my book, I kept in touch with happenings in Tobermory. Not surprisingly, Angus Black died at a healthy old age, and his son, Robin Black, took his place. I have corresponded with Robin and am pleased that the Western Isles has remained in good, solid hands.

Not long ago, I was listening to the radio and heard a song that Lachie and I first heard at the ceilidh at the Western Isles.

> *I'm yearning for my Hebridean island,*
> *The mountains there are heather sweet today.*
> *It may be just because my heart is Highland*
> *I long for Mull and Tobermory Bay.*
>
> *The birds need only lift their wings and wander,*
> *I wish I were as fortunate as they.*
> *If I had wings to spread I'd fly them yonder,*
> *And settle down by Tobermory Bay.*
>
> *My dream of Mull grows stronger still and stronger,*
> *So strong it is I dare not disobey.*
> *It's home for me, I can indeed no longer*
> *Resist the call of Tobermory Bay.*

Well, maybe I will return. Someday. With Gary—when the children are grown.

I remembered again those last moments with Angus on the Isle of Mull. Quietly, without a fuss, he packed Pauline's few belongings, so that no one there would become alarmed and begin a fruitless search. Most likely, he gave the clothes to a charity shop. I have no idea what happened to her house in London; Angus said that he would get in touch with the Council head and try to come up with a believable story.

Angus encouraged me to take whatever I wished. I still have some of Pauline's books. One is *Heidi*, which probably reminded her of those two happy years in Switzerland. Another is a slim volume of poetry, which contains a highlighted poem about Staffa by John Keats. I also kept her diary, poignant, heartbreaking. And, of course, I became the owner of the richest Armada treasure of all—a worn and tattered Sea Journal.

It had been almost time to take the bus back to where the ferry would start me on my journey home, but I still had one more thing to tell Angus. Something I had held back before, although I wasn't sure why.

"Before Pauline and John vanished, Angus, I saw something else. I saw John fasten a sprig of white heather into Pauline's hair."

Tears came into the dear man's eyes. Then he smiled. "Aye, that was the way it was meant to be. The bonny bride wore the lucky white heather."

Fact and Fiction about The Borrowed Days

THE BORROWED DAYS ARE A true Scottish legend and remain a superstition today. The weather on the last three days of March and the first three of April are problematic anywhere. In our country, we say that if March comes in like a lion, it will go out like a lamb. Both the Borrowed Days and the Lion/Lamb comparison are just two of many ancient weather superstitions. Most Scots place those suspicious days in March and April, although in some parts of Scotland, the culprits are late February and early March.

Recently, I learned of another Borrowed Days story—this one coming from Spain. Another Spain and Scotland connection! In the Spanish folktale, a shepherd promised March a lamb if March would make the winds gentle and protect the lamb. March agreed to the deal, only to have the shepherd change his mind. He would not give March the lamb. March was furious and sought revenge. It borrowed three days from April and used the extra days to create such miserable weather the shepherd lost his entire flock.

April Fools' Day is observed by many cultures and is older than Gowkie Day in Scotland. It might have begun as early as 1582 when the Gregorian calendar began. Not everyone got word and continued to use the Julian calendar, celebrating the New Year on April 1, rather than January 1. Those in the know laughed at them and considered them fools. In Scotland, the Day of the Gowk is a two-day observance. The Gowk means cuckoo, and the April Gowk is a fool. Often on the first day, people are tricked into going on fake errands. On the second, mischievous and often rude pranks are pulled.

Tobermory, Isle of Mull, is real, and a fine place for a visit, although perhaps not in late March or early April. One August, I stayed at the Western Isles Hotel and was thrilled to see a large poster advertising "I Know Where I'm Going" hanging over the fireplace. The movie, starring Wendy Hiller and Roger Livesey, is one of my favorites and the reason I chose the Western Isles.

The shops and houses of Tobermory along the pier are colorful. Boats go out often for seal and whale watching and tours to Iona and Staffa. The museum and aquarium mentioned in the novel are must-visits. Tobermory Chocolates is still packed with eager customers. Transportation on the island is relatively easy because of the fine bus service, although the narrow roads with passing places are best maneuvered by competent drivers.

Sir Lachlan Maclain, Laird of Duart Castle, works hard to keep the castle going. Keeping it in good repair and well heated is both a loving obligation and an expensive chore. The castle is as described in the novel, including figures of Spanish hostages in the dungeon. Fortunately, they do not move. Duart Castles's Tea Room is famous throughout Scotland.

Torosay Castle is no longer available to visitors, although the grounds remain open. The little steam engine has closed. Occasionally, there is talk of starting it again.

All characters in this book are fiction, although references are made to a few people who lived. There have been many Lachlan Macleans of Duart, but my young American Lachie is imaginary.

As far as the Spanish Armada goes, the basic background information is correct. What is uncertain is exactly which ship was the second Armada casualty in Scotland. Most of the wrecked ships of the Armada, desperately trying to return to Spain via the North Sea, were destroyed off the coast of Ireland. Spanish ancestors from that time, still in Ireland today, are sometimes referred to as "Black Irish," although historians discount this as another myth.

It is certain that a Spanish ship dropped anchor September 25, 1558 in Tobermory Bay, where it remained until it was blown up on November 5, 1558, curiously enough on Guy Fawkes Day, commemorating the attempted explosion of Parliament in 1605. Most people believe that the ship was the 800-ton Ragusan warship, the *San Juan de Sicilia,* with a crew of over three hundred. Others believe it was the *Valencia,* which was more likely to have treasure aboard—possibly thirty million gold ducats!

Did Donald Maclean, a young relative of Duart's Laird, light the powder keg and blow up the ship? That is the most popular legend. It is true that the Chieftain of Duart, Lachlan Maclean, offered food to the Spaniards if they performed a task for him and then paid the laird before leaving. While this doesn't seem generous, Maclean would have been within his rights to kill the Spaniards without offering anything. They were the defeated enemy, and those were not forgiving times. The Spaniards went to battle against the laird's enemies, the MacDonalds, and then tried to leave without making the agreed-upon payment. The story goes that Maclean was determined to get even.

Another theory was that the English, still fearing the Armada was a threat, sent an undercover agent aboard to destroy the ship. It is also possible the explosion was just an accident.

The story of the Lady of the Rock is a true legend of Mull, and you can see the rock from Duart Castle. Angus's fishy story and his version of the legend of the white heather are ones he made up himself, with a little help from the author. The other heather story is, well, another true legend. The author takes the blame for the dreadful poem about Admiral Drake. John Burgess is innocent.

About the Author

MARILYN LUDWIG IS A LONGTIME resident of Downers Grove, Illinois and a frequent visitor to the UK. *The Borrowed Days* is her eighth novel and the third one written primarily for adults. She is a member of the Society of Children's Book Writers and Illustrators (SCBWI).

www.ingramcontent.com/pod-product-compliance
Lightning Source LLC
Chambersburg PA
CBHW020620120726
47905CB00003B/867